That's what Jonathan should be focusing on. Instead, he's picking up Cedric, a mouse shifter who's running from the Beasts and happens to have information on what the Beasts' next step will be.

Cedric just wants to save his brother, who's still in the Beasts' hands. He knows he can't do it on his own, which is why he decides to keep the date of the attack on Gillham to himself unless they help him get Archie back.

Neither of them had planned on being each other's mate. Jonathan has to choose whether he'll be there for Gillham or for his mate, while Cedric needs to decide what's more important — saving his brother's life, or saving the lives of everyone in Gillham?

Jonathan
Copyright © 2020 Catherine Lievens
ISBN: 978-1-4874-3092-4
Cover art by Angela Waters

Published by eXtasy Books Inc or
Devine Destinies, an imprint of eXtasy Books Inc

Look for us online at:
www.eXtasybooks.com or www.devinedestinies.com

Jonathan
Council Enforcers 24

By

Catherine Lievens

CHAPTER ONE

Jonathan wasn't sure how to behave when it came to Devon. He didn't know the man, but he was one of his teammates' mates, so he was part of the family. It was strange to think of Devon with Elroy after seeing him with Lorcan, even though Jonathan was aware of the fact that Devon hadn't been with Elroy because he wanted to.

That made Jonathan want to strangle Elroy even more than he already did, which was a lot, since Elroy threatened his home and the people he cared about. The man needed to pay for what he'd done, and not just to Devon. Devon was worried sick about his friend, and Jonathan wanted to help. He didn't know how, though. He didn't know anything when it came to Devon, unfortunately.

"Relax," Tanner murmured.

Jonathan swallowed. "How can I relax? We know something's going to happen, but we don't know what or when."

"It's not going to help if you're nervous. For now, we don't know what Elroy's planning, and we have to wait. You can't be hypervigilant the entire time."

He was right, so Jonathan forced himself to smile and relax against the couch.

Lorcan and Devon had moved in together, and they'd invited the team to celebrate with them. Devon's cheeks were flushed with happiness, and it hurt Jonathan's heart to think that something might happen to him or anyone else in the house right now. Both Lorcan and Devon were worried, and so was he.

He got to his feet. "I'm grabbing another beer. Do you want one?" he asked Tanner.

Tanner shook his head. "I'm fine. Don't drink too much, though. I don't want to have to drag your ass back to the enforcers' building."

Jonathan rolled his eyes but didn't answer. Instead, he headed to the kitchen. He did want another beer, but more importantly, he wanted a moment to breathe. He knew all of them were nervous, even though they were trying to act as if nothing was happening.

Jonathan had just stepped into the kitchen when he heard someone behind him. He turned around, smiling at Devon. "You could have told me you wanted something else to drink."

Devon smiled back, but it was obvious he was nervous. Jonathan hoped he wasn't the one making him feel that way.

"I just want some water."

Jonathan leaned his hip against the counter. He suspected that was only part of the reason Devon had to hide in the kitchen. "Everyone loves you. You don't have to worry about the team."

"It's not that." Jonathan arched a brow, and Devon's smile widened. "All right. It's not *only* that."

Of course it wasn't. Jonathan knew as well as the others that Devon hadn't been alone when he'd gone back to Elroy. A friend had been with him, and Devon hadn't heard from that friend since then. "I'm sorry about Cedric."

Devon's eyes widened. "How do you know I was thinking about him?"

"I didn't know for sure. But you're worried, and I'd hoped it wasn't because of me."

"It's not. You and the other team members are Lorcan's family."

"He already has a family," Jonathan pointed out.

"But you're a second family. The way I see it, he can have two families. I'm not worried about you or any other team members, though. I'm worried about Cedric."

"Are *you* okay?"

"Physically, yes. But I can't stop thinking about Cedric and what's going on with him."

"Are the two of you close?"

"In a way. We were never friends. We couldn't afford to be, but we also couldn't afford to stay away from each other. I only had him, and he only had me, even though we knew that if anyone found out we were close, they would separate us, and they would do so as cruelly as possible."

"He hasn't tried contacting you?"

Devon shook his head. "Not as far as I know. I gave him Lorcan's phone number before he ran away, and I hoped he'd use it, but so far, I haven't heard from him."

"It doesn't mean he's not okay. He's on the run. It can't be easy, and he might be trying to protect you since he knows Elroy wants you back."

"I'm sure that's the case. There's more, though, and I wish I knew what it was."

Jonathan tapped his fingertips on the counter. He didn't know the entire story, even though he'd been debriefed. He wasn't sure *Devon* knew the entire story. "He didn't run away the first time you did?"

"No. He was still there. That's how they got me back. They hurt him."

"Do you know why he didn't run away?" Because it didn't make sense. Jonathan didn't understand why anyone would stay with Elroy and the men working with him. Devon hadn't wanted to, but he'd been abused. Still, he'd managed to escape, and as far as Jonathan knew, Cedric could have done the same. He hadn't, though. He'd stayed there, and he'd been used against Devon.

3

"He never told me. Again, we weren't friends."

"Do you think he went back?"

Devon paled. It was a feat, since his skin was already pale, and Jonathan hoped he wasn't about to faint. "I hope not."

"But you're not sure."

"I can't be. He hasn't called me. I don't know why he would go back, but then I don't know why he decided to stay. I don't know what to tell you. I wish I could do more for him, but if he doesn't contact me, I can't."

Jonathan hadn't wanted to stress Devon out, especially not today. He was sorry he had, but he was intrigued about Cedric and the reason why he would stay with Elroy. He had questions, but he knew now wasn't the time to ask Devon, and besides, he wasn't sure Devon would be the best man to answer them. "We'll help him if he contacts you," he promised.

Devon smiled again. "I know you will. Lorcan already promised that. You don't have to promise it, too."

"I just want you to be aware of it. You're part of our family now. If you want us to help, we will."

"I do. I don't know what's happening, but I know Cedric. He wouldn't hurt a fly. If he went back, there's a good reason for that, even though we don't know it."

"Maybe we can find out. Do you know anything about Cedric? Maybe his surname, where he came from?"

Devon frowned. "I don't know. I'd have to think about it. Our friendship wasn't exactly a normal one. We were thrust together because of circumstances. I don't know if we would have been friends if things had been different."

"It doesn't mean you don't know anything about him. Think about it. If you remember anything, tell Lorcan. In the meantime, we'll be ready to help if Cedric does contact you."

But Jonathan couldn't deny things looked dire. He only knew what Devon had told him about the mouse shifter, and since Devon didn't know anything else, neither did Jonathan. He wasn't sure why it was so important to him to understand what was going on with Cedric. He'd never even met the man. He'd been there when Lorcan had saved Devon, of course, but they hadn't stuck around. The place had been crawling with Beasts.

He'd never seen Cedric, and what happened to the man shouldn't bother him, but it did. Whatever was going on, Cedric had tangled with the Beasts and with Elroy, and it wouldn't be good for him. He needed help, and Jonathan was more than able to provide that help, as were the other enforcers. They were a team, and they would work together to make sure nothing happened to Cedric.

Cedric had to contact them first, though. They wouldn't be able to do anything until they knew what was going on and where he was. Jonathan hoped for Devon's sake that Cedric would call him, but he wasn't hopeful. He suspected the Beasts had managed to get their hands on Cedric again, or he'd gone back. There had to be a good reason for him to have stuck around, and Jonathan imagined that reason hadn't changed.

Maybe they should look into it. They could investigate whether or not Cedric had gone back to the Beasts. If he had, they wouldn't be able to do anything for him. If he hadn't, they might be able to help him.

There was nothing they could do now, though, and Jonathan forced himself to smile at Devon. "Everything will be okay," he repeated.

From Devon's expression, he was pretty sure neither of them truly believed that.

Cedric scuttered under the dumpster. He was hungry. Even though he ate a lot less in his mouse form, he still had to eat *something.* As a mouse, he might be able to fill his stomach.

He couldn't believe he was still here. The only thing he wanted was to run away from this place, but he couldn't. Rick still had his brother, and he would kill Archie if Cedric didn't go back. That was the only reason Cedric was still around. He wanted to save his brother, but he knew that if he did go back to Rick, he'd be abused again, if not worse. Rick wouldn't let him forget that he'd run away, even though he'd done so on impulse.

He shouldn't have. When Devon had told him to run, he'd obeyed. He'd *wanted* to run. He'd wanted to escape the pain, the abuse, the humiliation. Rick found pleasure in hurting him, and the only reason Cedric hadn't left sooner was Archie.

And now, Archie was in Rick's hands, and Cedric had no way to know what was going on. He prayed Rick wasn't hurting his brother. He wouldn't put it past the man, and if that happened, Cedric would kill Rick himself. It didn't matter that he was smaller and weaker. He would find a way.

But instead of thinking about that, he should focus on saving Archie. He didn't want to be hurt again, and he didn't want his brother to be hurt, either. That meant he had to get Archie out of there, but he was only one man, and a weak one at that. He needed help, but he didn't have anyone in the world except for Archie, and Archie couldn't do anything for him. As it was, Archie couldn't even do anything for himself.

Cedric peeked from under the dumpster. No one was around, but he could hear the sound of people moving in the building. It was full of Beasts, including Rick, and they were dangerous. There was no way he could go in there, not if he wanted to make it back out again. On his own, he couldn't do anything.

He wasn't entirely alone, though.

He'd memorized the number Devon had given him. He did

know whose number it was, even though Devon had told him it was his. It was hard to believe Devon had a phone. The two of them had been in the Beasts' hands for so long that it was strange to think about anything being theirs.

Devon was the only person Cedric could trust, other than Archie. Devon had made it out. He'd told Cedric that he'd met his mate, and Cedric knew the man had come to save Devon. He'd taken Devon away, and maybe, just maybe, they would be able to help. Devon had told Cedric to call if he needed anything, and Cedric did.

Still, he wasn't comfortable at the thought of calling Devon. He didn't want to make himself vulnerable, and he knew that was what would happen if he did. Devon and his friends would want explanations, and Cedric would have to give them some.

He didn't have a choice. He wanted his brother to make it out of this situation, and that meant contacting them.

The problem was that he didn't have a phone. He didn't have anything, not even clothes. He'd been in his mouse form since he'd escaped from the room in which he was kept with Devon, and if he wanted to use a phone, he had to appear like a normal human being. Walking around naked wasn't going to help with that.

He had to think. He couldn't stick around the warehouse the Beasts were using as their headquarters. He wanted to, because he didn't want to be far away from Archie, but it wasn't helping. He'd been hanging around since he'd run, and he hadn't been able to do anything.

But sticking around was the only reason he'd learned about Elroy's plan.

Elroy had been pissed when Devon had disappeared again, and he wanted revenge. He was going to take it out on the entire Gillham town, not just against Devon and his mate. The thought of him marching into Gillham and hurting the people who lived there terrified Cedric, even though he didn't know them. He didn't have to know them to be afraid for them. He knew what Elroy and the Beasts would do, and he wanted to stop it.

He wanted Archie back more, though.

Even if Devon and his friends didn't want to help him, Cedric knew he had valuable information. He could use that as leverage, even though the thought made his stomach churn. He didn't want to use people that way, but it was the only way for him to be sure the enforcers would help Archie.

But for now, Cedric had to focus on himself, because if he didn't make it, neither would Archie. He couldn't stick around, even though his brother was in the building.

He sighed, then, without looking back, he ran. He knew most of the Beasts were aware of the fact that he was a mouse shifter, and he wouldn't put it past any of them to try shooting him to stop him from leaving. Even if they weren't sure whether or not the mouse they were shooting at was Cedric, they wouldn't care. Rick would want Cedric alive to be able to hurt him, but the other Beasts wouldn't try to catch him, not when it would be easier for them to kill him.

Luckily, he managed to make it away from the warehouse in one piece. He was out of breath, and he soon stopped. He looked around, needing to find a phone. He wasn't that far away from the warehouse, but he didn't want to go even further.

There was a motel on the other side of the street.

Cedric swallowed. Maybe, if he managed to get there, he could sneak into a room and use a phone. No one would probably notice he was there, so he might even be able to shower. It wouldn't help with his lack of clothes, but it would be better than being dirty. He was still starving, and he doubted there would be any food, but there *had* to be a phone.

He hadn't spent time in motels, so he wasn't sure, but it

was his best bet. He would have to cross the street, though, and he hoped he wouldn't end up under a car as he did so. The night was falling, and there weren't a lot of people in this part of town. The Beasts were there, and no one wanted to hang around them. That was probably why the motel parking lot was empty except for one car.

Cedric neared the edge of the sidewalk and looked left and right. He couldn't see or hear any cars, so he took his chance and threw himself off the sidewalk. He ran until his lungs hurt, but he managed to get to the other side of the street without ending up splattered on the asphalt.

He didn't stop, though. He *couldn't* stop, not until he was in a safe place. He hurried toward the motel, looking around. The only car was parked in front of the room closest to the office, so Cedric headed the other way. He looked at the doors as he passed by, but all of them were closed. He would have to find a way inside one of the rooms.

Luckily for him, he had experience in this, and his mouse form was small and agile. It helped that one of the windows in a room at the back had been left slightly open. That way, he wouldn't have to hurt himself by trying to pass under the door or something.

He climbed the wall and snuck through the window, then dropped on the other side. He paused, waiting. Maybe someone was staying here, and that was why the window was open. He couldn't hear anyone, though, and when he looked around, the motel room was empty. There wasn't even a bag or anything, so he was pretty sure no one was staying there right now.

The room was like all motel rooms were—stained carpet, mismatched furniture, and lumpy pillows. It smelled stale, as if no one had stayed there in a while. Cedric hoped that was the case. He didn't care if the room was a disaster. It was still better than sleeping on the streets in his mouse form.

He shifted. It felt strange to be in his human form again, and he wiggled his fingers and toes. He wanted a shower desperately, but first, he had to call Devon.

The evening was winding down when Lorcan's phone rang. They all knew what that could mean, so they stopped moving toward the door and waited for him to answer.

Jonathan doubted it was work, since Lorcan's phone was the only one ringing, but still. Even though it was probably Lorcan's mom or his sister, everyone was on edge, and they wouldn't leave until they were sure everything was all right.

Lorcan took his phone out, stared at the screen for a second, and answered. "Hello?"

Jonathan tried to focus, but he still couldn't hear what was being said on the other side of the phone. Whoever it was, they were keeping their voice low, and it made him curious. It wasn't work, so Jonathan and the others probably should leave, but they were still hanging in the living room staring at Lorcan. They weren't going anywhere, not until they knew what was going on.

"I'm happy you called," Lorcan said. He listened for a bit, then nodded. "He's right here. I can give him the phone if you want, although if you need help, it's probably better if you speak to me. I can put you on speaker. My team is here, and we can decide what to do together. I know you don't trust us, but I hope you trust Devon."

There was a pause as Jonathan and everyone else in the room held their breath. Devon looked like he wanted to snatch the phone away from Lorcan, but he stayed where he was, wringing his fingers together and staring at his mate.

Lorcan finally lowered the phone. He touched something on the screen, then said, "You're on speaker."

"Cedric?" Devon asked. The word burst out of his mouth,

and he stared at the phone.

"Devon?" a voice asked.

Devon's shoulders slumped. "I'm so happy you called. I wasn't sure you would."

Cedric snorted. "Why did you give me the number, then? And why did your mate answer? I thought it was your phone."

"I knew you wouldn't call if I told you. I'm sorry. I shouldn't have lied, but I was panicking, and I wanted to be sure that you had a way to contact me. Where are you? What happened? We can come to get you. You just have to say the word."

Jonathan could tell that if Devon had his way, he would be out the door in seconds. Jonathan kind of wanted to go with him, but he knew that acting on impulse wasn't going to work. Cedric sounded wary, and it was understandable. Anyone would be in this situation.

"Cedric?" Sue asked.

There was a pause before Cedric asked, "Who is it?"

"My name is Sue. I'm a wolf shifter, and I'm the leader of this team. You're aware of the fact that we're council enforcers, right?"

"I am."

"All right. I'm happy you called. You need help?"

Cedric hesitated, and Jonathan held his breath. He wasn't sure how this would go. Everyone knew Cedric needed help, but that didn't mean he would be willing to accept it. He'd called, though, which meant something.

"I need help," Cedric confirmed.

Jonathan released the breath he'd been holding. This was the first step into getting Cedric what he needed.

"Can you tell me where you are?" Sue asked.

"I'm not sure. At a motel. I'm not far from the warehouse where the Beasts and Elroy are staying."

"Do you need someone to pick you up?"

"I don't—yes. I need to talk to whoever is in charge first, though."

"In this situation, that would be me. I do have to contact my superior to be sure he's okay with me sending someone out to get you."

"Good. I need to talk to someone who makes decisions."

"I'm sure that can be arranged."

Jonathan didn't understand what was going on, but the only important thing right now was that Cedric was reaching out for help and that they were going to give it to him.

"How long will it take you to get here?" Cedric asked.

"You can stay on the line while I call my superior. I can even put him on speaker if you want to talk directly to him, but I don't think he'll have a problem sending someone to get you. It's not going to be easy, though. You just said that you were still in the area where the Beasts are staying, and we can't afford for them to find any of our enforcers. It's dangerous."

"I'm aware of that," Cedric said, a hint of humor in his voice.

"Wait a moment. I'm calling my superior."

Sue stepped away from the group, her hand already in her pocket to take her phone out. Jonathan knew she was calling Bran, and hopefully, Bran would agree that someone needed to go get Cedric. He'd promised Devon that if he needed anything, he could count on them, and Bran was a man of his word.

Sue wasn't wrong, though. Cedric was in an area that was probably crawling with Beasts. Whatever had happened to Cedric for him to stick around, they had to know he wouldn't go far. They probably expected him to be around still, and Jonathan wouldn't be surprised if they were looking for him. They had other things to focus on, of course, but some people were obsessive, and apparently, the man who'd been abusing Cedric was one of those.

Devon hadn't gone into details, but he'd explained that just like Elroy had set his eyes on him and had decided he was his, the same had happened to Cedric. The guy who'd abused him was named Rick. Hearing the few details Devon knew, Jonathan wanted to get his hands on the man and tear his head clean off his body.

It wasn't long before Sue came back. "Cedric?" she asked.

"Yes?" Cedric answered. He'd been silent, so Jonathan was relieved to hear him.

"I talked to my superior. He agrees we can send someone to pick you up, and that we should probably stick to only one person. An entire team of enforcers will be too obvious. He's going to make a few phone calls."

"Can you come? Or maybe Devon's mate?"

"Our team is on break, unfortunately."

Dammit. Jonathan had forgotten about that, and he could hear from Cedric's tone that he wouldn't take this well. "I can go," he offered.

The entire team turned to look at him. Sue arched a brow, and Jonathan knew she had questions.

"Who is that?" Cedric asked.

Jonathan cleared his throat. "My name is Jonathan. I'm a team member, along with Devon's mate. I can pick you up if you want."

"I don't care who comes, as long as someone does."

"Jonathan?" Sue asked.

Jonathan knew she was the one he needed to convince, so he turned his attention to her. "I don't mind. I know it's dangerous, and I'll be careful."

"I'm sure Bran will find someone else, someone who's actually working right now."

"I'm sure he can. But I'm part of Lorcan's team, and even

though Cedric doesn't trust any of us, he knows Devon. Devon can vouch for me in a way he can't for other people."

Sue thought for a second. "Bran isn't going to be happy."

"I'm sure you can convince him this is the best way."

"Probably, although I'm not sure about that, either." She turned toward the phone Lorcan was still holding. "Would you be more comfortable with someone who's part of Lorcan's team?" she asked Cedric.

"I don't know. I don't know any of you. The only person I do know is Devon."

"And I vouch for Jonathan," Devon said. His eyes were wide as he stared at the phone.

"Then I'm fine with him. I just need someone to come. Please."

Sue nodded. "All right. I'll talk to my boss, although I doubt this will be a problem. Will you be safe for tonight, or does Jonathan need to come to you right now?"

Cedric sighed. "I guess I'll be fine for tonight. The motel room I picked is empty, as is most of the motel. I doubt anyone is going to come to this room tonight."

"Good. But if anything happens, I want you to call Lorcan again. We can be with you in minutes."

"I will." He hung up, leaving the entire team to look at each other.

Jonathan wasn't sure why he'd volunteered, but he wasn't going to go back on his word. He wanted to help Cedric, even if it meant going into an area full of Beasts. It would be a dangerous mission, but he was used to those, so it was nothing new.

Cedric truly didn't care who came to pick him up as long as someone came. Still, he felt better that Devon had vouched for the man who was going to come. He and Devon might not have been friends, but they'd been as close as they could have been in the situation they'd been in, and Cedric trusted him. He was one of the only two men he trusted, along with his brother, and it meant a lot.

The motel room phone started ringing, making him jump. He was still standing there, and he stared at it, wondering who it was. He didn't want to answer, but he was afraid that the ringing might make someone come, and he couldn't afford that to happen.

He picked up the receiver and brought it to his ear. He waited, wondering what was going on.

"Cedric?"

Cedric relaxed. "Devon. Why are you calling? How did you get this number?"

"I'm not sure how it works, but Lorcan was able to bring it up on his phone. Something about all the enforcers' phones tracing the numbers that call them or something like that. I don't know."

"You shouldn't have called." But Cedric was glad he had. He felt lonely, and even though he and Devon couldn't see each other right now, it was better to be on the phone with him than alone in this room.

"Lorcan did tell me that, but I had to check on you. You didn't say anything about how you were, and I was worried."

Cedric blinked. He hadn't expected Devon to be this worried about him, although he was relieved that was the case. "I'm fine." Or at least, he would be soon.

"I don't know if I believe that." Devon hesitated. "Why are you still in the area? When you ran away, I thought you'd leave. I thought you'd find a way to safety and start living your life. Yet you're still there."

Devon didn't know about Archie, and even though Cedric trusted him with his own safety, he wasn't sure he could trust him with his brother's. "I can't tell you."

Devon sighed. "I suspected that would be the case. Don't worry. Jonathan will pick you up tomorrow as soon as possible, and then, you can finally relax."

But he wouldn't be able to. He'd have to come back for Archie, and he had to make Devon understand that. "I also have info on Elroy's next step."

There was a pause. "What?" Devon asked.

"You heard me. I snuck back into the warehouse. I know where Elroy's office is, and I spied on him and the others. I know what he's going to do and when."

"Will he attack Gillham?"

"He will."

"When? I need to tell someone."

Cedric bit his lower lip. He felt guilty about not explaining himself better, but he couldn't. This was his only useful bit of information. He had to use it as leverage to get Archie to safety. He couldn't get his brother out of the situation on his own, and he needed the enforcers to do it for him. "I can't tell you."

"What do you mean, you can't tell me? The entire town is in danger. My *mate* is in danger. You have to tell me."

"Only if the enforcers agree to help me."

"Dammit, Cedric. We've already agreed to help you."

"I wasn't talking about picking me up and taking me away. I need to get back into the warehouse."

"What are you talking about? Why would you want to go back?"

"For the same reason I stayed for so long," Cedric snapped. He sucked in a breath. Yelling at Devon wasn't going to help.

"You never told me why."

"I know. There's a reason I didn't, and I don't want to explain this time, either."

"Is it because you don't trust me?"

"It's because I'm terrified."

Devon waited.

Cedric closed his eyes. "Rick has my brother."

"I didn't know you had a brother."

"Rick met Archie first. He didn't take him then, but after he saw me and I rejected him, he kidnapped Archie to use him as leverage against me. That's why I was with him and why I never tried to leave. I couldn't, not when Rick could hurt my brother. And now I ran away, and I don't even know what happened to Archie. I need to get him back."

"Of course you do, and we'll help you. You can trust me."

"I want to." But Cedric wasn't sure he could. It was terrifying, but he couldn't trust anyone except his brother. Devon wasn't his friend. They'd spent time together in a challenging situation, and they were somewhat close, but they still didn't know each other. What if the enforcers tried to get the information out of Cedric without helping him? It would be stupid to try to sneak into the warehouse. It was full of Beasts, and it wouldn't be smart for anyone to try to free Archie, not even them.

Cedric didn't care about smart, though. He wanted his brother back, and he would do everything he could to make that happen. He didn't like holding such an essential piece of information away from the people it would help the most, but if this was the only way to get Archie back, he would do it.

"But you can't." Devon sighed. "I understand. I'm sorry you feel that way, but I *do* understand. All right. I'll contact Sue and tell her what you just told me. It won't change the fact that the enforcers will try to help you, but she needs to know."

"I should have told her. I wasn't sure she would agree to help if I did, though. I know that this isn't a good thing."

"But you're ready to do everything you have to do to save your brother. I get it. I don't think less of you for doing this. I do wish you'd tell me what's going to happen, but that's because I'm terrified for my mate."

Cedric was relieved. "Thank you."

"It won't change anything, though. I know the enforcers will agree to help you, even if it's dangerous."

"I can't risk it. As soon as I have Archie back, I'll tell them." Although Cedric might have to explain sooner, because he didn't know how much time Gillham still had. He had no idea what today's date was, and no matter how he felt about this, he wouldn't sacrifice an entire town, not when he could help save it.

Cedric didn't want anyone to get hurt. He was using this information to get to Archie, but if something happened, he wouldn't hesitate to tell whoever was in charge what Elroy was planning. He wouldn't allow anyone to get hurt to save Archie. Archie would beat his ass if that happened, and he would be right.

But right now, Cedric had to focus on the fact that he might get his brother back. "I have to go," he said. Even though he wanted to spend the rest of the evening on the phone, he knew he had to sleep.

"All right. You can call Lorcan anytime you want or need, though. I want you to know that. He'll help you, even if he has to come on his own."

"Thank you."

"Stop thanking me. You're my friend. I want to do this for you."

Cedric's chest felt tight, and he hung up without saying goodbye. He stared at the phone for a second, expecting Devon to call again, and when he didn't, he was both dismayed and relieved.

He went to the bathroom. He didn't want to linger long enough to shower, not right now, so he just used the toilet, washed his hands and face, and shifted. He scampered into the room again, sneaking under the bed. He was used to sleeping in his mouse form, so it wasn't a hardship. Still, it was hard to fall asleep when he was terrified and excited at the same time.

Tomorrow, he would find out whether or not he would be able to save his brother.

CHAPTER TWO

Jonathan was ready to go. He was both nervous and eager to be doing something, especially since he'd be helping Devon's friend. Devon had been jumpy last night when Cedric had called, and Jonathan suspected he still was. He'd probably be on edge until Cedric was safe in Gillham, and Jonathan wanted to do that for him—and for Cedric. They'd gone through a lot, way more than any human being should go through, and it was a miracle Devon was doing so well. Of course, Jonathan didn't spend a lot of time with Devon, so it was possible he wasn't, but he was free and working on being happy with Lorcan, and Cedric deserved the same.

Sue had texted Jonathan to tell him that he'd have a meeting with her, Bran, and Kameron before going. He hoped they wouldn't tell him they'd changed their minds and that he had to stay in Gillham while they sent someone else to get Cedric.

He knocked on the door to Kameron's office. He could hear voices inside the room, but they stopped, and the door opened a few seconds later. Sue looked worried, but she smiled at Jonathan, so he figured things had gone okay with Bran and Kameron.

When Jonathan stepped in, he saw that Kameron was behind his desk, while Bran was standing close by. They both nodded at him, and Kameron gestured at the chairs on the other side of his desk. Jonathan wanted to go to Cedric, but he knew they needed to talk before he could, so he obeyed the silent order and sat.

"We agreed you could go get Devon's friend," Bran said.

Jonathan felt relieved. "When am I leaving?"

"As soon as this conversation is over. Your Nix team member will shimmer you to him. She doesn't have to stay if he's uncomfortable, but you will have to come back with her, so you'll have to talk to him. You'll be able to assess the situation better once you meet him."

"I will." Hopefully, Cedric would understand it was the only way they could get back to Gillham fast enough. Jonathan could vouch for Nadha, but he doubted that would help when it came to Cedric. The only reason he was allowing Jonathan to pick him up was that Devon had vouched for him, so it made things a bit more complicated.

"I'll try to explain, but he's understandably wary," Jonathan pointed out.

"We understand that, and we're fine with it."

Kameron cleared his throat. "I can't say I'm comfortable with the thought of having you so close to the Beasts, but we won't abandon Cedric. If you need time to convince him to come back with you, take it. You should probably feed him, at the very least, and Devon called us last night to tell us that Cedric had information about Elroy and his plans."

Jonathan blinked. "I didn't know about that. He didn't say anything during the conversation I heard."

Kameron nodded. "Apparently, he was planning on keeping that information to himself until we agreed to help his brother."

"I'm confused."

"Devon called him last night," Sue explained. "He was able to get the number from Lorcan's phone. They talked, and Cedric told him that he knew when Elroy was going to attack. He knows Elroy's plans, and we need them. The only way he's going to give them to us is if we agree to help his brother. The Beasts have him. They used him as leverage to keep Cedric with them. That's why Cedric never ran away and why he's still in the area."

"So he won't tell you anything unless you agree to help his brother?"

"He doesn't know we know. He told Devon, who was supposed to keep this information to himself until Cedric got here. Devon thought it was important we knew about it, though."

Jonathan agreed, but he was surprised Devon had called Kameron or Bran. Knowing the situation, he would have expected him to keep the secret to himself. Devon had left Elroy because he wanted to help Gillham, as well as because he'd been abused. Jonathan didn't know which one of those things had finally pushed him into leaving, and he didn't think it mattered. Devon was a good person, and he wanted to help Gillham. "Will you help him?"

Kameron nodded. "We would have helped him and his brother even if he didn't have the information we need. I don't think he understands that, though, so we need to get to his brother as soon as possible."

"Do you want me to stick to the area, then? I can try getting to the brother."

"It's too dangerous. We need you to bring Cedric here. From what Devon told us, he'll probably be in bad shape. At the very least, underfed. We need to feed him, make sure he rests, check his health, and talk to him. You can tell him we agree to help his brother and to give both of them a home if they want to stay here."

Jonathan was relieved. "Are you angry at him for keeping this information to himself?" Jonathan was slightly, but he understood why Cedric was doing it. Cedric didn't have anyone else but his brother, and maybe Devon. He certainly didn't trust anyone, and that included the enforcers. He probably thought that if he wanted his brother back, he would have to use something as leverage, and this information was perfect for that. Hopefully, if things came to it, Cedric would tell them even before they got his brother back, but Jonathan was going to do his best to get Cedric and his brother to safety.

He didn't like the thought of leaving Cedric's brother behind, but Kameron wasn't wrong. They needed to make sure Cedric was okay, and he was probably the only one who knew exactly where his brother was. It wouldn't be easy to get to him. Jonathan suspected that since Cedric's brother was being used as leverage against him, he was being kept in one of the Beasts' safe houses, and they would be crawling with Beasts. They'd also probably be shielded against Nix, so they wouldn't be able to enter that way.

The situation was becoming more complicated by the minute, and Jonathan was almost afraid of what he'd find when he got to Cedric.

"Nadha will be waiting for you at the enforcers' house," Sue said. "She already knows what's happening. I briefed her earlier. She's aware of the fact that she'll have to shimmer you there and come back here to wait for a call from you to get you back. She doesn't like it any more than any other team member, but we know it's for the best." She hesitated. "You have to be careful. If at all possible, try to stick to the motel where Cedric is staying. He knows how to avoid the Beasts, and can probably recognize them by sight. You don't know them as intimately, and you might need his help. Try to convince him to come back here as soon as possible, but we're all aware of the fact that it's not going to be easy. He's understandably afraid and worried about his brother. He'll need to trust you before he agrees to come here."

Jonathan nodded. "I can do that."

Sue finally smiled. "I know. I wouldn't have agreed to let you go if I didn't think you could. Be careful and protect both yourself and Cedric."

Jonathan had his orders, and there wasn't anything else to say. He had to get to Cedric, make sure he was okay, and convince him to come back to Gillham.

Piece of cake.

Jonathan left the office and Kameron's house to head to the enforcers' house. Just like Sue had said, Nadha was waiting for him when he got there. She didn't look happy, but she didn't try to change Jonathan's mind. Neither did the other team members who had gathered in the living room. He looked around, and he couldn't help but smile. "I'll be fine," he promised.

Lorcan snorted. "You can't promise that."

"I promise I'll be as careful as I can, though. I know it's weird to go on a mission on my own, but I can do this."

"Be careful," Tanner said.

Jonathan could only nod and turn to Nadha. She nodded, and they headed out the front door toward the spot from where she would be able to shimmer them out.

"I don't like this," she said.

"Neither do I, but I have to do it."

"Come back in one piece. I don't want to lose any team member, and that includes you."

Jonathan smiled. "I promise I'll do everything I can to make that happen."

She sighed, but she offered Jonathan her hand, and he took it. The forest around them disappeared, and Jonathan sucked in a breath. He was going to get Cedric back, and hopefully, Cedric's brother, too.

Cedric had been waiting by the motel room window. He wasn't sure what to expect, but he hoped Devon had really sent someone. Cedric wasn't sure what he would do if his friend hadn't. Probably run and keep hiding for a while.

Eventually, the Beasts would have to leave the warehouse, and that would be his best bet to get to his brother. It would also mean the Beasts were attacking Gillham, though, and Cedric's stomach churned at the thought.

He didn't want anyone to get hurt. Archie would kick his ass if he let it happen, but he didn't have any other leverage to get the council to help him get his brother back. Besides, he wasn't planning on holding back the information if they couldn't help him.

He needed help, though. He didn't know if he would get it, but he hoped Devon and his friends would keep their word, which was why he was standing in the motel room, still staring out the window. He was hidden by an old curtain that had once been white, and he hoped it would be enough to shield him.

How would whoever was coming get here? Gillham was far away, so they would probably use a Nix. Would it be a normal one, or one who worked with the council enforcers? Cedric had a lot of questions and zero answers. He needed them before he agreed to leave this place, though.

He wasn't stupid. The council didn't know about the information he had yet, but they would insist he go back with whoever was coming to pick him up as soon as they found out. They'd want to make sure he was healthy and probably to feed him. They'd no doubt get angry and try to convince him to tell them what he knew, and he would, eventually. First, though, he would extract a promise from them to help Archie. That was the only thing he could do, and he wasn't backing down. He didn't care if Archie hated him after this was over, as long as his brother was safe.

A movement in the parking lot made him jerk back. He narrowed his eyes, staring at the man who'd come from somewhere around the motel office. He wasn't wearing a uniform, but Cedric recognized his stance. He was glancing around, obviously looking for something — or someone. Cedric suspected the man was his ride out of here, but how could he be sure?

He should have asked Devon what Jonathan looked like. As it was, he was going to have to open the door, and he didn't trust this guy. He didn't recognize him, but that didn't mean he wasn't a Beast. Cedric had spent a lot of time at the warehouse, but there were a lot of other safe houses the Beasts used, and he didn't know every single recruit.

He needed to do something.

He stepped away from the window and turned toward the phone. The only thing he could think of doing was calling Devon and ask him what Jonathan looked like. Once he knew, he would be able to tell whether or not the guy outside was the person he was waiting for. Hopefully, Devon would answer.

He did. "Cedric? Everything okay?" he asked.

"I'm fine. There's a guy here, and I'm not sure whether or not he's your friend. Can you describe him for me?"

"I should have thought about doing that sooner."

"It doesn't matter. I just need to know what Jonathan looks like, please."

"He's tall, probably around six foot two or three. He has dark hair cut short and dark eyes. Brown."

That described the guy outside, but also about half of the male population in the country. "Anything else?"

There was a sound as if someone was taking the phone away from Devon, so Cedric wasn't surprised to hear Lorcan's voice. "Cedric?"

"Yes?"

"Jonathan is wearing a pair of jeans and a black t-shirt."

That helped a bit. Although, he supposed the guy outside could still be dressed the same way as Jonathan as a coincidence. "So you're positive it's him?"

"I am. He just left pack territory, so it would make sense. We can stay on the line while you talk to him, though, if it makes you more comfortable."

It was tempting, but Cedric didn't need anyone to hold his hand. "It's fine. Just, if you don't hear from me, you'll know I've been kidnapped."

"And we'll come get you. Don't worry."

Cedric was touched, but he was also still worried.

He hung up, then looked through the window to where Jonathan was standing in the middle of the parking lot, waiting. He didn't look angry or impatient. He was just looking around and waiting.

Cedric grabbed the sheet from the bed and wrapped it around his naked body before taking a deep breath and quietly unlocking the door. The slight sound got Jonathan's attention right away. His head snapped toward Cedric, and he stared.

Cedric opened his mouth, but Jonathan shook his head and held a finger up. Then he stepped away, and Cedric hoped that finger meant that he wanted Cedric to wait.

Cedric closed the door and obeyed. He had no idea what Jonathan had in mind, but he didn't think the man would leave without him. The council had promised they would help him, and he wanted to trust them. It was hard, though. He didn't trust anyone but Archie, and maybe Devon. He wasn't entirely sure about him, either.

The next five minutes were the longest in his life. He sat on the edge of the mattress, staring at the window and waiting for Jonathan to come back. When he did, Cedric's shoulders slumped, and he relaxed. He still didn't know what Jonathan had in mind, but at least he hadn't left without him.

He moved toward the door again. Jonathan was standing just outside of it, waiting, and Cedric didn't want either of them to garner attention, which meant he had to let him in.

He unlocked the door and slightly opened it. "Who are you?" he asked. If this wasn't Jonathan, he wouldn't know the name of the person Cedric was waiting for.

"My name is Jonathan. I'm a friend of Devon's, and I work for the council." Jonathan's voice was steady and serious, but he sounded calm and sure of himself. It made Cedric want to trust him.

"You're here for me?"

"I am. Will you let me in?"

"If you want. Shouldn't we be leaving, though?"

Jonathan hesitated.

Cedric shielded himself for whatever bad news he was about to hear.

"I thought we could spend the night here," Jonathan explained. "I went to the office and rented this room. It's obvious you don't trust me, and I didn't expect you to. This way, there will only be one person you don't trust. Or we can go to Gillham. Whatever you're more comfortable with. If you want Devon, that can be arranged, too."

Cedric frowned. "Wouldn't it be safer for both of us to leave the area as soon as possible?" Cedric didn't want to, but it was what he'd expected would happen.

"It would. I don't want to freak you out, though. I don't want you to have to force yourself to do anything else. We can go if you want, or we can stay in this room. As long as you don't leave it, it shouldn't be a problem. The Beasts don't know me, so I can go grab you some food and clothes. I suspect you'll be more comfortable shimmering back to the Gillham pack if you're dressed."

Cedric hadn't even thought about that, and he was touched that Jonathan had. He'd been spending so much time in his mouse form that it was more comfortable for him to stick to that. He didn't want to, though. He wasn't just a mouse shifter. He was also a man, and he didn't want to feel vulnerable.

Staying here for the night would mean trusting Jonathan, though. They would have to share the room. Cedric didn't know how that would work, but Jonathan wasn't wrong. Cedric would feel more comfortable if he could stay here tonight, get dressed, and eat something.

He had to make a decision, and he didn't know which way to go.

Jonathan knew that staying the night was a risk, but he could see Cedric was freaking out, even though Cedric hadn't said anything about it. He was trying to appear strong, and Jonathan was impressed, but it didn't mean he didn't want to make things easier for Cedric.

He hadn't known what to expect when he'd thought of the man. Maybe someone similar to Devon. He was shorter, though. Both of them were slight in that way people who didn't get enough food were, so that was something they shared. Cedric's brown hair was too long and hung in front of his brown eyes. He kept looking around as if he expected someone to jump out and attack him. Jonathan would put him in his mid to late twenties, which was older than Devon, although not by much.

Cedric and Devon also shared that hunted look. Devon had slowly been losing it, but it was obvious in Cedric's eyes, and Jonathan wanted to do something about it. It was one of the reasons he wasn't dragging Cedric back to Gillham. He would have to contact Sue and explain what was going on, but hopefully, Sue would agree that this was the best thing they could do. She, Bran, and Kameron had known it was a possibility, after all.

Jonathan knew the situation was time sensitive. Cedric had the information they needed, but they would get it only once they helped Cedric's brother. Cedric also had to trust them, and the best way to make that happen was to go along with what he wanted and how he felt. Besides, Cedric needed a good night's sleep and food, and possibly, a shower. He also needed clothes, and Jonathan was more than happy to provide those.

"You should get a shower now that the room is officially ours," he said.

"What will you do in the meantime?"

"I'll go buy some food and clothes. That way, you won't have to hang around naked or in your mouse form. We can talk more then."

Cedric looked like he wanted to protest, but instead, he nodded. "You'll have to knock when you come back. I'll lock the door."

"That won't be a problem."

Cedric looked surprised, and it made Jonathan wonder what kind of people had been in his life until now. He already knew the answer to that, though. If Cedric had been with the Beasts for any length of time, it meant that the people he'd lived with were assholes. Knowing that they'd forced him to stay using his brother made Jonathan want to kill someone, and hopefully, he would have the opportunity to do it when he met the Beasts.

Right now, though, he had to focus on Cedric and on making him comfortable.

Jonathan handed Cedric the key and turned around. He could feel Cedric's gaze on his back, but he didn't look back, no matter how much he wanted to. For whatever reason, he was fascinated by Cedric, and he wanted to see what was going to happen next. He wanted to protect him and make sure nothing bad happened to him ever again, and he didn't know whether or not he would be able to do that.

The area wasn't great, but Jonathan managed to find

everything he needed. He stuck to simple clothes, buying jeans and plain t-shirts, as well as underwear, socks, and a pair of trainers. He hoped he'd gotten the size right, but he would only find out once he got back to the room. As for the food, Cedric hadn't told him whether or not he was allergic to anything or if there was anything he didn't eat, so Jonathan had gone for burgers and fries.

He went back to the room, slightly wary about what he was about to find. He wanted Cedric to be okay, but he didn't know if that was possible, not with everything happening. Cedric had been forced to stay with the Beasts for months, if not longer. His brother had been there, too, and it had to have been hell for both of them.

It wasn't surprising that Cedric was using the bit of information he had on Elroy to get his brother back. Jonathan might have done the same if he'd been in his shoes, and he couldn't blame him. If anything, it made him want to protect Cedric even more. He knew that some people wouldn't like what Cedric was doing, and Cedric had to feel guilty about it. It couldn't be easy to hold people's lives in his hands — hell, an entire town — and decide to use it as leverage.

But Cedric didn't know that the council would have helped him even if he hadn't done this. He didn't trust anyone, not even the council, and that was one more thing Jonathan couldn't blame him for.

Jonathan's phone vibrated in his pocket, and he realized he hadn't let Sue know what he was doing. He swore and quickly took the phone out of his pocket, juggling the bag that contained Cedric's new clothes and the one filled with food. "Hello?"

"You haven't called Nadha yet. Why? What's going on?" Sue asked.

Jonathan didn't know what was happening in his brain, but he had to get his head straight on. "I'm sorry. I found

Cedric. He's okay, at least as far as I could see."

"Good. There's still something going on, though."

"He's afraid. Wary. He seems to be physically okay, but he's hungry and needed a shower and clothes."

"We can provide all of that as soon as he arrives here."

"About that. I think it would be a good idea to keep him here for at least one night."

Sue was silent for a moment, and Jonathan prayed she saw things the way he did. "I suppose we expected it," she said.

Jonathan swallowed. "I know I should have called you. When I got here and he opened the door, he was wearing the sheet that had been on the bed and nothing else. He has this haggard look to him."

"He's been spending all his time in his shifted form."

"I suspect that's the case, yes. He's also terrified. He doesn't know I'm aware of the situation with his brother, and he obviously doesn't trust me. He doesn't trust the council, either. I thought that showing him I was trying to help would help him relax."

"Staying is dangerous, though. You're right in the middle of the Beasts' territory. What do you think will happen if they find out you're there?"

"They won't. They don't know me, and I'm not wearing my uniform. Besides, now that I have food and clothes for Cedric, I'm not planning on leaving the motel room until tomorrow. I want to try to convince him that the council will help his brother even if he tells us what's going on with Elroy. We need that information, and we can't afford to wait for it."

"And you think that staying there with him on your own is going to help?" Sue sounded skeptical.

Jonathan felt the same way. "It can't hurt. Like I said, I'm not planning on leaving the room, and neither is he. But this is neutral ground. He won't feel as trapped as he might in pack territory. He has no reason to trust any of us, and I hope this will show him that we only want to help."

Sue sighed. "All right. I'll let Kameron and Bran know. I don't like this, but you're there, so you know better than me. Keep in touch, though. I want to know if anything happens, and I can have Nadha to you in minutes."

"We'll be back tomorrow."

"I hope you're right. I don't want either of you to get hurt. Besides, we have to talk to Cedric."

"I know." Jonathan didn't know whether he should bring up the fact that Cedric was using this information as leverage to him. Cedric would probably freak out, because no one but Devon was supposed to know, and Jonathan didn't want to put a wedge between the two.

Still, it might be the only way to get answers. Jonathan somehow doubted that even once he got Cedric to pack territory, he would talk. He wanted his brother back, and he had something the council would be eager to get. If he was smart — and he had to be to stick around this area and avoided being recaptured by the Beasts yet — he wouldn't say anything until his brother was standing in front of him.

Cedric tensed when someone knocked on the door, even though he knew it had to be Jonathan. He held the sheet he'd wrapped around himself after his shower tighter and peeked through the window, pushing the curtain to the side. Jonathan stood there, holding two plastic bags, and when he noticed Cedric, he beamed at him.

Cedric withdrew and blinked. He had no idea what was going on in Jonathan's mind, and he wasn't sure he wanted to find out. The man confused him, and he disliked feeling that way, especially in his situation.

He unlocked the door and peered out, just in case. He was surprised when Jonathan didn't try to push his way in and instead waited for Cedric to allow him in. He didn't even look impatient.

"I got food," Jonathan said. He held one of the bags out.

The smells coming out of it made Cedric's stomach rumble. He stopped resisting. He still wasn't sure whether or not he could trust Jonathan, but as it was, he didn't have a choice.

He opened the door and grabbed the bag from Jonathan's hand. Jonathan let go with a smile. Cedric stepped back and went to sit on the bed, already looking in the bag. The food was wrapped, but he'd recognize the smell of a cheeseburger anywhere.

He barely looked up when he heard the door close. Jonathan was inside now, and he looked around. Cedric focused on the cheeseburger, unwrapping it and giving it a bite. He closed his eyes and groaned, trying to remember when he'd last eaten something this good.

When he blinked his eyes open, Jonathan was staring at him. It made Cedric realize what he must have sounded like, and he had to look away. Luckily for him, it was easy to distract himself with the food.

"This doesn't look great," Jonathan said as he looked around again.

Cedric snorted. "It's a rundown motel in a bad area of town. What were you expecting?"

Jonathan wrinkled his nose. "I suppose you're right. Did you shower?"

It took Cedric a moment to chew and swallow the food in his mouth. "I did."

Jonathan nodded and came closer. "Well, I have clothes for you once you're done eating. I wasn't sure about your size or what you'd want to wear, so I stuck with jeans and plain t-shirts. I also bought a pair of shoes, socks, and underwear."

He was close enough to touch by now, and he leaned closer to drop the bag onto the bed.

Cedric didn't know what happened, but one second, Jonathan looked normal, and the next, his eyes widened and he took a step back.

Cedric frowned and tilted his head to the side to smell his armpit. "I told you I showered. I wasn't crazy about the soap I found in there, but I don't think I stink anymore." Jonathan continued staring. Cedric was sure he didn't stink, and he didn't know what was going on. He took another bite, still looking at Jonathan and trying to understand him. "So? Do I stink?"

Jonathan cleared his throat. "It's not that."

"What is it, then? You look like you've seen a ghost. I might not have eaten in a while, but I'm not *that* pale."

"You truly don't know, do you?"

"What are you talking about? You can explain or stop acting like I have an enormous spider on my forehead." Cedric paused and tilted his head. "Wait. Is that what's going on? Do I have something on my forehead?"

Jonathan laughed. Cedric grinned at him, having obtained what he'd been looking for.

"There's nothing on your forehead," Jonathan said. "That's not what's going on." He hesitated, then moved closer again. "You should smell me."

He offered his wrist, and Cedric stared at it. Why was Jonathan suggesting this? It didn't make sense. "Do you want me to find out whether or not you stink?" he asked.

"I know I don't stink, and neither do you. Just smell me. You'll understand."

"You can't just explain like a normal person?"

Jonathan huffed, but he was smiling. "I can, but I know you'll want proof."

Cedric stared at his burger, then at Jonathan's hand. He sighed and wrapped the burger again, hoping he'd be able to get back to it soon. He put it back in the bag and reached for

Jonathan's arm. He brought it closer, sticking his nose to the inside of the wrist, and took a deep breath.

It hit him. Now, he understood what Jonathan was talking about.

He dropped Jonathan's arm as if it had burned him and stared at him with wide eyes. "You should have told me," he said.

Jonathan arched a brow. "Would you have believed me if I had?"

Probably not. Still, Cedric would have liked a little warning that his mate was standing in front of him.

He didn't know what to do with this. He couldn't deny Jonathan was his mate, but he didn't know him. He didn't know if he could trust him, and he didn't have the luxury or time to deal with it. It complicated an already complicated situation even more.

He sighed and reached for his burger again. "I don't know what to tell you."

"I don't expect anything from you. I know this is far from being the ideal situation to find your mate."

"You're right, and there's a lot more to it than you know."

Jonathan rubbed the back of his neck. "Actually, I think I know everything there is to know."

"Trust me. You don't."

"I know about your brother. We all do. The council agreed that he needs to be saved."

Cedric froze in the act of raising his burger. "What do you mean that you know about my brother?"

"Devon told Kameron, the Gillham pack alpha. You don't have to worry about it. He just wanted the council to know what was going on and to make sure they would help you."

Cedric felt betrayed, but he also understood why Devon had done it. He probably would have, too, if he'd been on the other side of the situation. He should have known Devon would do this, but he supposed it helped him. This way, he didn't have to tell the council about his brother anymore. They already knew, and they would help, or at least, that was what Jonathan seemed to think.

"What did they say? Do they know what kind of information I have?"

Jonathan nodded. "They do. They're aware of the fact that you know when and where Elroy is going to attack, and they want to find out."

"That's why they agreed to save my brother."

"They would have helped your brother regardless. I know you don't trust them, but I know them. I know Kameron since I live in Gillham. Even if the council had refused to help you, he would have."

"Because he's the Gillham pack alpha. He stands to lose a lot if the town is attacked."

"And because he's a good man. I promise you we'll help. Hell, if it comes to that, I'll go wherever your brother is and drag him out myself."

Cedric blinked. "You're only saying that because you want to get in my pants."

Jonathan barked out a laugh. "Do I have to point out you're not wearing any pants?"

Cedric shrugged. "That doesn't matter. I'm your mate, and you want to fuck me." If he was honest with himself, he wouldn't mind fucking Jonathan, either. It had been so long since he'd had sex he actually wanted to have, and even though he didn't know Jonathan, he could tell Jonathan wouldn't force him. Of course, that could merely be the mate bond and fear talking.

Cedric *wanted* to trust Jonathan. He wanted to believe his mate would always treat him right, but he knew better. Besides, even if he wanted to fuck Jonathan's brains out, he had to focus on Archie. Once he had his brother back, he could think about having sex with his mate.

"So you know about Archie."

Jonathan frowned. "That's a weird twist in the conversation. Who's Archie?"

"My brother."

Jonathan nodded. "I do. I'd like to hear about the situation directly from you, but I suspect you probably need to sleep."

"I slept the night away."

Jonathan's expression softened. "I have no doubt you *tried* to sleep. I don't know the details of the situation, but I can tell that you've been on the run for a while. I doubt you're well-rested, and now that you've had a shower and food, I want you to get into bed and try to sleep some more. You don't know me, and you don't trust me, but I swear to you I won't let anything happen to you."

He was right. Cedric didn't trust him. He was exhausted, though, and now that he was eating, he could feel his eyes slowly sliding shut. It wouldn't take long for him to fall asleep if he didn't fight it. "Why? Is it because I'm your mate?"

"And because you're Devon's friend. You have no reason to trust me, but you're going to have to. I can promise you that I won't hurt you as many times as I want, but it's not going to change the situation. You have to take a risk."

Cedric didn't want to, but he knew he was already taking a risk when it came to Archie. The council hadn't done anything to help him and Devon, but they hadn't known about them, and as soon as Devon had managed to escape, they'd welcomed him into their ranks. It could be because he was a council enforcer's mate, but then, so was Cedric.

That was going to take some time to get used to.

He sighed. "Fine. I'll go to sleep."

Jonathan smiled. "Good. I'll stand guard. You don't have to worry about anything but getting some rest. Then, tomorrow, we'll head to Gillham and talk about what's next for you and your brother. But I promise you, even if I have to go on my own, I *will* get Archie back for you."

Cedric didn't know why, but he found himself believing Jonathan.

CHAPTER THREE

When Jonathan woke up the next morning, he spent the first five minutes staring at his mate. He supposed he shouldn't be surprised that he and Cedric were mates and destined to be together. His entire team had started meeting their mates, and he was one of the few left who hadn't. It was a coincidence, but he still should have expected it at the rate things were going. He'd been more focused on keeping Cedric safe, though, although even that made sense now. He might not have met Cedric before, but it seemed like his bear had already known they were mates, and it had wanted to keep Cedric safe.

It was one of the reasons Jonathan was sleeping on the floor. Cedric had fallen asleep yesterday morning after Jonathan had arrived, and he'd spent most of the day and the night in bed. He'd woken up when Jonathan had brought in dinner, and he'd even offered half of the bed to Jonathan, but Jonathan had refused. He could see Cedric was still wary, and he understood why. They might be mates, but that didn't mean Jonathan was a good person. Cedric was already trusting him a lot, and that was good. The rest would come later. Besides, they had other things to focus on.

Today, they were going back to Gillham, and hopefully, in the next few days, they would get to Cedric's brother. Jonathan was tempted to go now, but he knew better. He was only one man, and even with Cedric, he wouldn't be able to get to Archie.

The few times he'd left the room yesterday, he'd seen how

many Beasts were around. They didn't do anything that screamed they were criminals, but they all had the same insignia on their jackets, and Jonathan had fought enough of them to know what they usually looked like. The area was full of them, and he could only imagine what it would be like at their headquarters.

Getting Archie by himself was impossible, no matter how much Jonathan wanted to. That meant he and Cedric had to go back, and he knew Cedric wasn't happy about that, even though he'd agreed. Cedric wanted to rush in and free his brother, and Jonathan wanted to do it for him. Instead, they were headed back to Gillham. He supposed he should be lucky Cedric hadn't protested more than he already had.

Jonathan's bear was pushing for him to wake Cedric so they could talk about their relationship. They didn't have one yet, and he doubted they would have one anytime soon. He wasn't going to push. Cedric needed time, and Jonathan didn't have a problem with him focusing on his brother before focusing on their relationship. Archie was in danger, while they would have all the time in the world to get together. Besides, it wasn't just Archie. Jonathan was focused on his own job. He needed to protect Gillham and the pack, and that had to take precedence. It was hard, though. Both he and his bear wanted nothing more than to wrap Cedric in their arms and make sure no one ever hurt him again.

Cedric was strong, though. He was stubborn. He wouldn't allow anyone to coddle him, not even Jonathan. He'd managed to escape from the Beasts, but instead of running away like anyone would have, he was still there. It was impressive, even though Jonathan wished he hadn't had to do it.

Jonathan rose from the floor. He stretched his back, hoping that tonight, he would be able to sleep on something softer. It wasn't the first time he'd slept on the floor—the team had gone on a few missions in which they'd been in the middle of nowhere, and they'd had to make do — but usually, he shifted. He hadn't last night because he didn't know what would happen or whether the Beasts would find them. The last thing he needed was for someone to see a bear and freak out.

He grabbed the pillow he'd been using and put it on the bed next to Cedric. Cedric rolled over almost immediately, reaching for it, and Jonathan was surprised when he hugged the pillow to his chest and took a deep breath. He seemed to relax after that, and Jonathan stared for a few moments longer. Even though Cedric had pushed him away, it looked like he found comfort in Jonathan's scent. It made Jonathan feel better.

He headed to the bathroom, then once he'd washed up, he decided to go get breakfast. Since he didn't want Cedric to freak out, he left him a note. Once that was done, he headed out.

He made sure to be attentive to his surroundings as he headed to the diner he'd found yesterday. The waitress smiled at him when he stepped in, and he made a beeline for the counter. "Can you make breakfast takeaways?" he asked.

"Of course. Just tell me what you want and wait here."

While he was waiting, Jonathan decided to call his team leader. Sue was probably worried out of her mind, and besides, he had to tell her that Cedric was his mate. He didn't know if it would change anything, but she needed to know, and so did the others.

"Jonathan. You're still alive," she dryly said when she answered.

Jonathan chuckled. "I told you we were okay. Don't tell me you worried the entire night."

"You know I did. Are you coming back today?"

"Yes. Cedric spent yesterday sleeping. I had to wake him up to get some food into him, but I'm sure he'll feel better today."

"We'll still have Dallas check him out. Is there anything else?"

Jonathan briefly closed his eyes. "There is." He looked around to make sure no one was listening in to the conversation, but no one seemed to care. All the customers were focused on their breakfast, just like he and Cedric would be soon. "Turns out that Cedric is my mate."

Sue was silent for a moment. Then, she asked, "You're not joking, are you?"

"I wouldn't joke about something like that. Believe me. I was surprised, too. I didn't realize until he let me inside the room after I grabbed lunch."

"Right. How do you feel about it?"

"I'm not sure yet. We haven't really talked about it. He's focused on helping his brother, and I understand."

"How does *he* feel about it?"

"I don't know. He didn't seem horrified, if that's what you're asking. We didn't have time to talk, though."

"You'll have more time today."

"He's anxious about his brother. Apparently, a man who wanted Cedric used Archie as leverage. He's still being held by the Beasts. I'm pretty sure this guy wants to use Archie to get Cedric back." And that wasn't going to happen. It wouldn't have happened before, but there was no way Jonathan was allowing anyone to touch his mate, not unless Cedric was okay with it, and he very much was not in this situation.

"I hate that people do that, but I'm not surprised. We know the Beasts."

Jonathan nodded. "We do. I'm grateful that the council will help."

"They wouldn't have said no. Even if Cedric wasn't your mate, they would have helped."

"I know. I'm grateful we'll be able to do something."

"It won't be easy, but then, when have our missions ever been easy?"

Jonathan laughed. Just then, the waitress came closer, holding a bag. He smiled at her and took the bag, then headed out. "Well, I got Cedric and me breakfast, and I'm headed back to the room. I'll be home soon, and we can talk more then."

"All right. I'll send Nadha to you in about an hour. She'll be in the spot where she shimmered you. Don't be late."

"We won't be." Jonathan couldn't wait to be out of the area. He knew that staying for one night had been necessary for Cedric, but he wasn't happy about it. He didn't like being hypervigilant, and it was what he was doing right now. He needed to protect Cedric and himself, and that meant being attentive to his surroundings. Beasts were crawling everywhere, and the less he saw of them, the better he would feel.

He and Sue hung up, and he made his way inside the motel room. He wasn't surprised to see Cedric was still sleeping when he got there, so he started taking the food out of the bags. He was pretty sure Cedric's stomach would wake him up eventually, and if it didn't, well, Jonathan would do it. He was looking forward to spending some time with his mate, even though he still wasn't sure how Cedric had taken the revelation. He wasn't sure it mattered, either. He wasn't about to push for something Cedric wasn't ready for. Knowing his mate made him feel good, though, and he enjoyed taking care of Cedric.

He hoped Cedric would enjoy having someone taking care of him after all the time he spent with the Beasts.

Cedric frowned when he smelled coffee. Usually, when he woke up, he was kicked out of bed, or worse. He'd woken up many times with Rick in the bed with him wanting something other than breakfast. Besides, no one ever took care of him. If he wanted to eat, he had to go downstairs to the kitchen and grab something with the Beasts watching. It was one of the reasons he was so thin. He didn't eat much because he didn't want to face any of them. He was scared, but he hated them so much that he was also afraid of what he would do if he got his hands on any of them, especially Rick.

No one was touching him right now, though. Even though he could hear Jonathan moving inside the room, Jonathan didn't try to wake him up. Cedric knew that he and Jonathan had to move, yet Jonathan wasn't pushing him to go faster, and that was strange. But no matter how much Cedric wanted to stay in bed and sleep the day away like he had yesterday, he knew they needed to move.

He blinked his eyes opened and looked around. Jonathan was turned away from him, focused on something on the tiny table under the window. The curtains were drawn, so no one would be able to see them from outside.

Cedric was relieved to have a moment to observe his mate. He still had a hard time believing he'd met Jonathan and that they were linked that way, and he wanted more time to explore the bond. He hoped that once they had Archie back, they would have that time. He knew better, though. Jonathan was an enforcer, and with Elroy planning on attacking Gillham, he would have his hands full. The attack was going to happen soon, and Cedric felt guilty about not telling the council about it. He was pretty sure he should now. Jonathan had promised he would get Archie back, and for whatever reason, probably because of the bond they shared, Cedric believed him.

"Good morning," he said as he sat up. Dwelling on those thoughts wouldn't help right now. He had to focus on getting stronger, eating, and helping both Archie and the Gillham pack.

Jonathan turned around. "Good morning. Did I wake you

up?"

"It was the smell of coffee."

Jonathan smiled. "Well, there's plenty of it. You can have mine if one is not enough."

Cedric shook his head, bemused. "I don't want your coffee. I'll take mine, though."

"Good. Why don't you use the bathroom? I'll get everything ready in the meantime."

Cedric would have been suspicious if anyone else had told him that, but he forced himself to obey. He knew he'd hurt Jonathan by not falling into his arms yesterday, but also that Jonathan wouldn't ask or push for anything. He would let Cedric do things at his own pace, and Cedric was relieved. After being forced to do things that he didn't want to do for so long, he wanted a bit of respite.

He was only half surprised that Jonathan was that way. He'd always known Rick was an asshole, so he hadn't been surprised at what Rick had done to him. Jonathan was different, and Cedric found himself wanting to get to know him better. He would, in time. Right now, they both had other things to focus on.

When he left the bathroom, the small table was laden with food. "Did you buy half the food at the diner?" he asked.

Jonathan rubbed the back of his neck. "I wasn't sure what you liked or what you wanted, so I decided to get a bit of everything."

He wasn't kidding. Cedric could see bacon, eggs, toast, pancakes and waffles, oatmeal, and even pie. "I doubt I'll be able to eat all of that."

"Eat whatever you want and however much you want. I just wanted you to be able to choose."

Cedric grabbed the plastic fork that had come with breakfast and held it tight. Jonathan probably didn't realize how important that was to Cedric. It was only breakfast, but

Jonathan was giving Cedric a choice, something he hadn't had in too long. "Thank you."

"Don't worry about it and start eating. Someone is coming to pick us up in an hour."

Cedric's stomach churned. He was worried about meeting the enforcers and the council. "Who am I supposed to talk to later? The entire council?"

Jonathan sat on the edge of the mattress and shook his head. "You'll only be talking to Kameron and Bran. Bran co-ordinates the enforcers, but he's based in Gillham. He often helps Kameron when it comes to the council and the Gillham pack security. Since the danger is to Gillham and the pack, Kameron will take the lead. He'll keep the council up to date with whatever is happening, but he's in charge."

Cedric was relieved. Still, even though he knew he had to talk to Kameron, he also didn't want anyone to forget about Archie. "When are we going to get my brother?"

Jonathan grimaced. "I'm not sure. I know you want to go right now, and if we could, I'd agree. There are too many Beasts, though, and even though I'm sure you know your way into whatever place they're keeping your brother, it's too dangerous. Besides, you might be able to sneak around, but I can't. I'm a bear shifter. It's not exactly inconspicuous."

Cedric imagined it wasn't. He was disappointed that he wasn't saving Archie today, but he understood. He wouldn't be able to help Archie if he was captured again, so even though his instincts were to go right now, he stayed where he was. Archie had been in Rick's hands for too long, but Rick wouldn't hurt him, not the way he had hurt Cedric. Cedric had to cling to that knowledge and try to forget what was happening to his brother for the moment.

"But they'll help?" he asked before stuffing a bite of waffle in his mouth.

"They will. We need a plan, though, which is one of the

reasons we're going back to Gillham."

"We don't have time."

"We'll have to *make* time."

Cedric tightened his hand around the fork. Even though he was trying to focus on what was right, it was hard. He wanted to save Archie. He'd always felt guilty about Archie being taken by the Beasts. It was his fault, because Rick had wanted him and Cedric had rejected him. That was why Rick had decided to use Archie as leverage, and now Archie was stuck. Cedric owed it to him to get him out of this situation and to do it as soon as possible.

Jonathan leaned forward, startling Cedric, who'd been lost in his thoughts. "I know how you're feeling," Jonathan said softly. "Trust me. I understand. You want to bring down the world to save your brother, and if there was a chance to do it and survive, I would go with you. This is an impossible situation. By leaving Archie behind, you probably feel like you're abandoning him. You're not, though. It won't do him any good if you get hurt, but if you come to Gillham with me and put together a team? We'll have even more chances to get him back."

Cedric wanted to say no, but he couldn't. He'd tried to help his brother on his own, but he hadn't been able to do anything. He needed help, and now, he had it. He didn't like that it meant going along with whatever Jonathan and the others wanted, but he didn't have a choice. It was either that or going back for Archie on his own, which would no doubt end up badly. Even if Rick didn't catch him, another Beast could, which was terrifying. At least Rick was the evil Cedric already knew.

He was going to have to do what Kameron wanted him to do. He wouldn't have a choice in this situation, either, and the thought made him tighten his hold on his fork, almost snapping it in two.

He didn't want anyone to take his choices away, not even the council.

Jonathan had known how hard this would be for Cedric. He knew Cedric's first instinct was to go after his brother and help him, but it was the most dangerous thing Cedric could do. The risk of him being taken by the Beasts again was too high, and Jonathan wasn't willing to compromise, not when it came to Cedric's safety. If he had to, he would drag Cedric out of here. He didn't care if Cedric yelled, screamed, or threatened him.

He wanted to help Archie as much a Cedric wanted to, but he had to keep his cool. He was an enforcer, and he had to think like one. Cedric, on the other hand, only thought as a brother. It was understandable, but it was wrong.

"What will happen if you try to get him back on your own?" he asked.

"I don't know. I haven't tried yet."

"And *why* haven't you tried?"

Cedric's expression was stubborn. "Because I was tired. Because I was hungry."

Jonathan arched a brow. "Not because you knew it would be impossible?"

"Nothing is impossible. I know the warehouse. I know where Archie is kept."

"What if he's been moved? Do you really think that the guy who kept you there will keep him in the same place now that he knows you're out? He took your brother for this reason. If you want Archie back, you're going to have to give yourself up. You'll have to sacrifice yourself, and even though I don't know your brother, I'm sure he won't be okay with that."

Cedric continued to stare.

Jonathan had to find a way to make him understand.

"Besides, even if you do give yourself up, can you be sure that guy is going to keep whatever promise he made you?"

"Rick never made any promises. He isn't a promise kind of guy."

"But you know he'll do it if it means getting you back. He'll tell you whatever you want to hear, and then, once you're with him again, he'll ignore everything."

"You talk like you know him."

"I don't, but assholes are all the same. He took what he wanted, even though you didn't want to give it to him. He used your brother as leverage. The way I see it, he doesn't deserve to live, but you won't be able to do much against him on your own. If you could, you would have done it a long time ago. You'd have gotten your brother out of there, as well as yourself. Instead, you stayed."

Cedric sighed, and his shoulders slumped. "I know that what you're saying is true. If I go on my own, both Archie and I will end up dead or worse, and I don't want that to happen. It's hard, though."

"I know. But you're not alone anymore, Cedric. You don't have to do everything on your own. You should take advantage of the fact that me and the pack, and my team, will do everything we can to help you."

Cedric stared at Jonathan for a moment. "It's hard to wrap my mind around that. I've never really had anyone, not the way you're describing."

"Where are your parents?" Jonathan wasn't sure it was a good idea to ask, but even though they didn't have much time, he wanted to get to know his mate. They were still eating breakfast, and they had almost half an hour to get to the meeting point. It was more than enough time to ask a few questions.

Cedric turned his attention back to the food. "My mother died when I was a teenager. Archie is five years younger than me, and I was left taking care of him. My father, well, after my mother died, he turned to the bottle. He was in so much pain that he couldn't resist. I'm not even sure he noticed that Archie and I are gone. I'm not sure whether or not he still alive."

"I'm sorry you didn't have anyone. You do now, though."

Cedric smiled. It was a tiny smile, but it was better than nothing. "I know. But Archie and I have been relying only on each other for years."

"How old are you?"

"Twenty-eight. He's twenty-three, and he's my baby brother. He's in trouble because of me, and I hate myself for what happened."

"He's not in trouble because of you. He's in trouble because of the asshole who kidnapped him. I'm sure he's aware of that and that he wouldn't want you to get hurt to save him. From what you say, the two of you love each other. You're family, and you want to do the best you can."

"He would kick my ass if he knew I was holding back information for his sake," Cedric murmured. He poked at his waffles, but he looked like he wasn't hungry anymore.

"Well, I can't say I agree with what you're doing, but I understand, too. You don't trust us. Nothing is going to make that happen except time, and we don't have that luxury. It means we're going to have to find a compromise, and I hope we'll be able to."

Cedric looked at Jonathan. "Do you have brothers? Someone for whom you would do anything, even things you wouldn't be proud of?"

"I have two sisters. I also have a lot of friends, including my team. I consider all of them brothers and sisters. And yes, I would do anything for them, even things that are against the law or that I would hate myself for doing. If it meant saving them, though, I would do them."

Cedric stared for a second. "Then you understand?"

Jonathan sighed. "I do. I also understand that by going on your own, you would fail. I understand that you need the enforcers, or at the very least, me."

"Can't just the two of us go?"

"I'd feel better if I had my team at my back, considering the number of Beasts crawling around town. And I don't blame you for withholding that information." He was relieved that Cedric seemed to dislike it as much as he did, though. It meant Cedric was doing it only because he felt he had to, not because he was evil and wanted to.

Jonathan suspected that if Archie wasn't still in the hands of the Beasts, Cedric wouldn't have hesitated to give the information to Kameron. As it was, he felt like it was his only way to get his brother back. Jonathan couldn't be angry at him for that, and he doubted anyone he was close to would be. Even Kameron wouldn't push. He wanted to keep the pack safe, but he would never hurt Cedric in any way, be it physical or mental, to do it.

The situation felt impossible, but they had to focus on what was next. They were going back to Gillham, and Cedric would meet with Kameron and probably Jonathan's team. He would explain the situation once again, and they would plan. They were good at it. It was their job, and Jonathan couldn't wait. He wanted to kick Beasts' asses, but he wasn't a fool. On his own, he would probably end up dead. Together with his team, though, they would be able to get Archie out of there, and hopefully, to maim the Beasts enough that they wouldn't be able to attack Gillham.

"I hate that I'm doing this," Cedric murmured.

"You don't have to. I know it's going to take you more than my words to know that, though, but I can't promise you no one will push. We want to know what you know, but we won't hurt you to get that information. We wouldn't be better than the Beasts if we did."

"A lot of people will get hurt if I don't tell anyone about this."

"You have to make a hard choice, but I want you to know that I'll support you whatever you decide. You'll never be alone again, Cedric. Even if you decide you don't want me in your life, I'll always be there for you." It was the truth, although Jonathan hoped that Cedric wouldn't decide to disappear once this was over.

He wanted a chance to be with his mate. He wanted a chance at the almost perfect happiness he'd seen his teammates find. If Cedric didn't want that, though, he would let his mate go.

Cedric was both surprised and relieved that Jonathan seemed to understand what he was going through. He'd expected to be insulted, maybe to be forced to reveal what he knew. Instead, both Jonathan and the people Jonathan knew seemed willing to let Cedric do whatever he wanted. Cedric didn't understand it, but he didn't care what the reason behind it was. He thought they weren't smart if they didn't try to get information out of him, but he realized he was jaded from everything that had happened to him in the past few years.

Maybe the council and Kameron really weren't like Rick and the Beasts. Maybe Cedric would be able to have a future, something he hadn't allowed himself to wish for lately. It would have been too hard when he'd been with Rick, but now, he was free, and his thoughts soared.

He didn't have the time to focus on it, though. If he wanted Archie back and to help the Gillham pack at the same time, he needed to hurry. He had to go back to the pack, tell them what he knew about where Archie was, and hope they would rescue him. Once that was done, he would tell them everything he knew.

Or maybe he would tell them sooner. He didn't trust anyone yet, except for Archie and Devon, and maybe Jonathan, but he wanted to. He didn't want to keep this information to himself. It felt heavy in his chest, and that was because he knew it was wrong. He wouldn't let things go too far, though. If Kameron couldn't or wouldn't help him, he would tell him about Elroy anyway. He would never forgive himself if he didn't and people died because of him, and neither would Archie.

"If you're done, we should clean up, and you should get dressed. Nadha will be here soon."

Cedric turned his attention to Jonathan. "Who's Nadha?"

"She's my Nix team member." At Cedric's confused expression, Jonathan smiled. "Every enforcers' team has at least one Nix and one human. The other members are a mix of different shifters, from birds to bears, wolves, and lions, whatever you can think of. I'm a bear, Nadha is a Nix, while Sue, my team leader, is a wolf shifter."

"And you considered them family even though they're so different from you?"

"I do. I would die for any of them, and I know the same goes for them. We've been working together well. I wasn't always part of that team, but now I am, and I never want to leave."

"You're lucky to have so many people who care about you."

Jonathan's expression softened. "They will care about you and your brother, too. You just have to give them time and a chance."

Cedric wasn't sure he could do that, but it looked like he wouldn't have a choice. If he wanted to be with Jonathan, he would have to accept the people who came with him.

He still didn't know what he wanted, and he wasn't ready

to think about it, not when Archie was still in danger. He wasn't hungry anymore, so he put his fork down and got to his feet. "I'll go get dressed." He was only wearing underwear and one of the t-shirts Jonathan had bought for him, and even though he wasn't uncomfortable, he knew he couldn't exactly go to the pack dressed that way. Jonathan was one thing. The Gillham pack was another. "I'll help you clean up once I'm done."

Jonathan shook his head. "Don't worry. I'll take care of it. Take a little time to yourself. I doubt you'll have much of that once we head to the pack."

He probably wasn't wrong, but Cedric didn't want to waste time. He went to the bathroom again, brushed his teeth with his finger, and put the jeans, socks, and shoes Jonathan had bought him on. Once he was dressed, he stared at his reflection for a moment.

He didn't hate the way he looked, but he wished he were different. He wished he were stronger, and that he'd been able to protect his brother. Instead, he'd allowed Archie to be taken, and this was the situation they were in now.

Cedric straightened his back and squared his shoulders. He might be weak, but he could do this. Like Jonathan had said, he wasn't alone anymore, and he would take advantage of that. Besides, was it taking advantage when the people he was doing it to were okay with it?

He pushed away from the counter and opened the door. Everything that had been on the table was gone, and Jonathan was waiting for him. Jonathan smiled, and Cedric found himself smiling back.

This was strange for him, but he was relaxing in Jonathan's presence. He was still tense, and he suspected he would be until he knew Archie was safe, but in the meantime, this was good. He'd been hyper-focused and worried for so long that it felt weird not to feel that anymore. Right now, he could put his safety in Jonathan's hands, and he knew Jonathan would do whatever he could to help. It was strange, but also a relief.

"Ready to go?" Jonathan asked.

Cedric nodded, even though he wasn't. He didn't want to leave. He didn't want to be so far away from his brother.

He didn't have a choice.

He and Jonathan left the room. Jonathan popped into the office for a moment, but he was back only a minute later, and together, they walked down the parking lot until they reached a spot where no one in the office would be able to see them. A woman was standing there, staring at them. She wasn't wearing a uniform, but Cedric knew she was Nadha. Her long blonde hair was braided behind her back, exposing her pointed ears, and her green eyes had a worried expression in them. She smiled when she saw Jonathan, and Jonathan quickly hugged her when he and Cedric got to her.

"Ready?" she asked, clearly eager to be out of here.

Cedric nodded, and when she offered him one of her hands, he took it.

Then, he was gone.

It was only a second, and the parking lot they'd been standing in had become a forest. Cedric blinked and looked around, curious, but also wary.

"You've never shimmered before?" Jonathan asked.

"No. It was strange." It was even stranger to think that he was so far away from Archie now, and that it had only taken a second.

Something squeaked, and Cedric looked around, but before he could understand what was happening, something heavy slammed against him. He stumbled back. He was lucky that Jonathan was standing there and held him up. Arms wrapped around his neck, and he looked at Devon, who was now hanging from him.

His eyes widened. He and Devon hadn't been friends.

They couldn't afford to be. Yet here Devon was, crying against Cedric's chest. Cedric had no idea what to do, so he gently patted Devon's back. "I have no idea why you're crying," he said.

Devon laughed and looked at him. "I don't know, either. I didn't think I would. I just wanted to welcome you here and make sure you felt okay and safe, but instead, look at me. I'm a mess."

He took a step back, and a man Cedric hadn't noticed came closer. He put his arm around Devon's shoulder and pulled him close, kissing his temple, and Cedric knew he had to be Devon's mate. Looking at them made him wonder if he and Jonathan would have that eventually. He hoped so.

Jonathan cleared his throat. "If you're ready, Kameron and Bran are waiting for us."

Cedric turned his attention to him. "I don't think I'll ever be more ready than I am right now."

Jonathan stared at him for a moment, then nodded. "All right. But tell me if you need anything. If you're overwhelmed, if you want to leave, anything. I know that technically, Kameron gives the orders, but when it comes to you, I'm ready to go against them if it makes you happy."

Cedric blinked at the declaration. "Why? We just met."

"It doesn't change the fact that we're mates. We don't have to talk about that right now, though. Come on. They're waiting for us, and the sooner we do this, the sooner we'll have a plan in place and will be able to get to your brother."

Cedric had to focus on that. Everything else could and would have to come later. Right now, only Archie was important.

CHAPTER FOUR

Even though this was far from being an ideal situation, Jonathan wanted to make sure Cedric was comfortable. He was in a new place, where he didn't know anyone but Devon and Jonathan. He had to feel awkward, and he had to be terrified for his brother. Yet here he was, holding his head high, looking around.

Jonathan knew that the Gillham pack was kind of legendary to shifters. Kameron was the reason they'd had to come out to the humans. He'd shifted on video, and they hadn't been able to put the cat — or in this case, the wolf — back in the bag.

Curiosity was warring with fear and exhaustion, though. Cedric wanted to go back. Jonathan didn't have to ask him to know that. He wanted to get to his brother and make sure Archie was okay, but he couldn't. He was willing to use the information he had as leverage, even though he felt guilty about it. He was being pulled in so many directions, and Jonathan wished he could do something for him.

Maybe he could. He couldn't help as much or in all the ways he wished, but he *could* protect Cedric and make sure nothing happened to him right now. He didn't think anyone would attack him, but it would be too easy for someone to try to push him to tell them what was going on with Elroy without giving him anything in return. Cedric wasn't a bad person. He *wanted* to tell Kameron what Elroy was planning. He wanted his brother back more, though.

They made their way to Kameron's house, Devon and

Lorcan trailing behind them, while Nadha had gone back to the enforcers' building. Jonathan wasn't sure whether they would stay for the meeting, but if Devon's presence helped Cedric feel better, he wasn't about to protest. He hoped no one else would, either. Devon knew how Elroy thought, so he could be a precious source of information when it came to the man. Lorcan wouldn't be happy, because he wanted Devon to forget all about his past, but this was a war. Elroy was going to attack Gillham, and they couldn't afford to hide their head in the sand.

"This place is huge," Cedric murmured.

"You've never had a pack?" Jonathan asked him.

Cedric quickly smiled. "I'm not a wolf."

"So? No one here cares what kind of shifter they live with. Kameron is a wolf, and so are many of his pack members, but there are also bears, felines, and even a shark."

Cedric's eyes widened. "How does that work? We're in the middle of a forest."

"He has a saltwater pool. I'll show it to you sometime."

Cedric stared at Jonathan for a bit, then, to Jonathan's surprise, he nodded. "I'm looking forward to it."

It made something in Jonathan's chest flutter. Cedric was looking forward to spending time with him once all of this was over. He couldn't wait, but they had to focus on Archie and Elroy first.

"Kameron is a good alpha," Devon said. "He welcomed me even though I'm human and I was with Elroy. He won't hurt you."

Cedric shrugged. "I don't really care if he hurts me, as long as he helps me."

"I wish I'd known about your brother. I could have tried to help."

Jonathan blinked. He'd forgotten that no one knew about Archie until recently. Cedric had kept a secret, even from

Devon.

Cedric shook his head. "You couldn't have done anything, just like I couldn't."

Jonathan could tell Devon wanted to push, but thankfully, he didn't. They stayed in silence the rest of the way, and Jonathan desperately wanted to reach for Cedric. He wanted to hold his hand and make sure he was okay, but he didn't know whether or not the gesture would be welcome. Cedric wouldn't push him away, but he might not be comfortable with it. They didn't know each other, and the situation was complicated.

Thankfully, they reached Kameron's house quickly. Kameron was waiting for them, and he opened the door only seconds after Jonathan knocked. His gaze went from Jonathan to Cedric, and he smiled. "Cedric. It's a pleasure to meet you."

Cedric cocked his head. "Is it? You know what I'm hiding. I don't understand why you'd want to meet me. Unless it's to convince me to tell you what I know."

Devon sucked in a breath, but Jonathan kept his focus on Kameron. He was curious to see how the man would answer, even though he already knew Kameron's position when it came to Cedric.

"I do want to convince you to tell us what you know," Kameron agreed. "It's vital for the pack, and for the town. I'm not going to force you, though, especially not when the solution is so easy."

Cedric snorted. "There's nothing easy about this situation, but fine. I guess you want to talk to me?"

"I do. Follow me to my office."

They obeyed, trailing behind him down the hallway. Kameron's mate, Zach, peeked out from the kitchen and smiled. "Does anyone want anything to drink?" His gaze settled in Cedric. "Or to eat?"

Jonathan almost laughed. Zach was the alpha mate and a

caretaker. Jonathan knew he hadn't always been, but he was perfect. He took care of people, never ordered them around. That was Kameron's job.

Cedric seemed confused. "Water?" he asked.

Zach's smile was easy. "Right away. You sit down and relax."

Cedric leaned closer to Jonathan. "I don't understand. Why are they so nice to me?"

"Because they're nice people. I already told you that, but I understand why you didn't believe me. I hope you do now."

Cedric wrinkled his nose. "I'm not sure yet. They might be acting because they want to know what I know."

"I promise you they're not, but you're right. You don't have to believe me."

Cedric looked at Jonathan. "I think I do, though," he murmured.

Jonathan couldn't stop smiling as they walked into the office. He knew that Cedric believing him was a huge step forward, and he was happy about it. Now he just had to get Archie back, and of course, they had to defeat Elroy. Then he and Cedric would finally be able to get to know each other as mates.

"Sit down," Kameron said. He walked around his desk. "And tell me what happened to you. I only know bits and pieces, and I want to hear the entire thing."

Cedric sighed and sat into one of the chairs. "I'm getting tired of repeating myself, but fine. I met Rick, but I didn't know he was a Beast. He tried to get me to go out with him, and I refused. I didn't like him, even though I barely knew him. He struck me as a dick, and I was more than happy to stay away from him. He kept trying, but when he realized I wasn't going to say yes, he kidnapped my brother. He forced me to be with him and move in with the Beasts using Archie, and I want Archie to be free. It wasn't fair to him, and it still isn't. He shouldn't be suffering for something that's my fault."

Devon sucked in a breath. "How can you say it's your fault? Rick has been abusing you for a long time. I never understood why you stayed with him, but now, I do. You should have told me. We could have tried to find your brother."

Cedric shook his head. "We wouldn't have been able to. I know where Archie is, but I was never able to get him out. Rick made sure of that." He turned his attention back to Kameron. "When the Beasts started working with Elroy, Rick quickly climbed the hierarchy. Now, they work closely together."

Kameron nodded. "Is that how you found out about Elroy's plans for Gillham?"

"It's not. Well, not entirely. But since Rick and Elroy are so close, he moved Archie and me into the warehouse Elroy was using as his headquarters. I know the place. Once I escaped, I was able to shift into my mouse form and sneak back in. I knew where Elroy's office was, and it was easy to go there and listen to their conversations. That's how I found out when he's planning on attacking Gillham."

There was a moment of silence as they all considered Cedric's words. Jonathan wanted to ask what Rick and Elroy were planning, but he knew Cedric wouldn't answer. He thought Kameron was going to ask, but instead, he surprised him.

"So you know where your brother is?"

"I know where he was. They could have moved him, although I hope they haven't."

Because if they had, Archie would be impossible to find. If they couldn't find Archie, Cedric wouldn't tell them what Elroy was planning, and a lot of people would get hurt.

This was an impossible situation, and Jonathan wasn't sure there was a way out of it, or at least, not a way in which everyone would be safe — or even alive.

Cedric had no idea what to make of Kameron. The alpha seemed nice, and he wasn't hurting Cedric, which was a plus. He could be faking it, though. Cedric had seen enough of that to know that some people were good actors, especially when there was something they wanted. Unfortunately, the only thing he could do was trust Kameron. It was the only way to get Archie back.

He snuck a glance at Jonathan. Well, maybe. Jonathan had promised that even if Kameron refused to do anything, he would help, and Cedric had to believe that. He didn't want his mate to be a liar, not when he was already starting to trust him.

It would be too easy to fall in love with Jonathan. Even though they'd only met yesterday, Cedric felt drawn to him. That could be explained by the bond, of course, but it wasn't just that. Jonathan was taking care of him in a way no one had since Cedric's mom had died. He hadn't said anything about it, but Cedric had noticed.

Jonathan had bought him food. He'd bought him clothes, shoes, everything he needed. Once they'd arrived in pack territory, he'd made sure Cedric was okay. Cedric had no doubt that if Kameron or anyone else did anything to upset Cedric, Jonathan would step in.

Cedric supposed it made sense. Jonathan was an enforcer, a protector, and he was protecting Cedric.

Cedric didn't mind. He wanted to be protected. He'd always been the protector when it came to his brother, and while he didn't want that to change, he knew he'd done a poor job. He didn't want to hold the weight of their world on his shoulders anymore. He wanted someone to hold it with him, to share a burden, and he thought that Jonathan could be that person.

But first, they had to focus on Archie. Cedric prayed the pack would help. He felt so guilty about keeping the date of the attack to himself, but he didn't have a choice. Until Archie was safe, he had to do this.

"I'm so sorry," Devon murmured.

Cedric was surprised he was still there. He'd expected Devon to tell him he was a horrible person for keeping that information to himself. Instead, Devon looked like he was about to cry.

Cedric cleared his throat. "You don't have anything to be sorry about."

Devon shook his head. "I should have known something was wrong. I never understood, but it was obvious."

"Stop worrying about that. There's nothing you could have done anyway. What I have to focus on right now is helping Archie."

"I agree," Kameron said. Cedric turned to look at him. "If you're okay with it, I'd like to bring in the council enforcers' supervisor, as well as Sue, Jonathan's team leader. Together, we can plan how to get to your brother."

"Why would you do that?"

Kameron didn't look surprised by the question. "Because you asked me to. Because your brother is in danger, and no one should be in that situation."

"I know something that could save your pack and the town. I should be telling you, but instead, I'm keeping it to myself to force you to help me. You could beat me up until I confessed."

Kameron looked horrified. "Is that what you expected me to do?"

Cedric shrugged. "Kind of. Jonathan kept telling me you wouldn't, but I wasn't sure I could trust you, or him."

"Well, I won't touch you. No one here will. You're safe, and you don't have to be afraid. And we *will* help you save your brother. I wish you would give us the information, but I understand why you won't. You don't have a reason to trust me or anyone else. I hope you will in time and that you'll tell us, but even if you don't, we're already preparing for an attack. We'll fight Elroy, and we'll win. You don't have to worry about us."

But Cedric *was* worried. He felt like shit about keeping this secret, and he was tempted to blurt out everything. He wanted to help. He wanted Kameron to defeat Elroy and to make sure the man never hurt anyone again.

Archie would kick his ass when he found out about this. Cedric couldn't bring himself to tell Kameron everything, though. He'd been trying to get his brother back for so long. It felt like it would never happen, but he had a chance with Kameron and the pack. He couldn't waste it.

"Bring in anyone you want," Cedric told Kameron.

Kameron nodded and reached for his phone. Cedric leaned back in the chair he was sitting in, closing his eyes. Even though he'd slept for an entire day and night, he still felt exhausted. He could probably sleep for a week, but instead, he had to focus on what was happening.

"Do you need anything?" Jonathan asked in a whisper.

Cedric looked at him. He appeared worried, something that Cedric didn't fully understand. Cedric was his mate, but they didn't know each other. Why did Jonathan care so much already?

Cedric also didn't understand why he felt the same way. For whatever reason, he wanted to bury his face against Jonathan's chest and fall asleep there. He wanted Jonathan to keep him safe while he was unconscious, and when he woke up, he wanted everything to be perfect, for Archie to be back in his life, and maybe for them to live here. He wanted Elroy and Rick to be gone.

He sighed. "I'm fine."

"Zach will be here with your water soon. If you need anything else, just let me know."

"I don't need anything. I don't want to annoy anyone."

"You wouldn't. Zach is the alpha mate. It's literally his job to take care of people."

"It's his job to take care of pack members. I'm not a pack member."

"That's not how it works," Kameron said.

Cedric hadn't realized he was listening in, but he wasn't surprised. "What do you mean?"

"Zach takes care of everyone, pack member or not. It's not just pack members who live here, but also council enforcers."

"Well, I'm neither of those things."

"No, but you're Jonathan's mate. That means that you're one of us, one way or another."

Cedric heard Devon suck in a breath, but he didn't turn to look at him. Instead, he kept his focus on Kameron. "How can you say that when you know what I'm hiding?"

"Because you're hiding it for the right reason. I'm sure that as soon as we save your brother, you'll tell us."

He was right. Cedric only hoped they would get Archie back soon, because there wasn't much time left. If they didn't, well, he would have to tell Kameron about Elroy's plan anyway. He wouldn't be able to live with himself if people died or got hurt because of him.

Thankfully, the door opened, and he was able to distract himself from those thoughts. A man and a woman came in, and Kameron quickly explained the situation to them, even though Cedric was sure they already knew. Jonathan had told him he'd told his team leader that Cedric was his mate and about Archie. That meant they could go straight to the point, and Cedric couldn't wait.

"Where's your brother kept?" the man asked. He had to be

Bran.

"In the headquarters, where Devon and I were when Devon came back."

"Would you be able to get to him?"

"Yes. I did go to him, but I was in my mouse form. I wasn't able to help him." But he would now. He had help. He wasn't alone anymore, even though it was hard to believe.

Bran nodded and looked at Sue. "What do you think?"

"As long as Cedric can draw us a plan of the place, it should be fairly easy. I suppose they have Nix blockers?"

"They do. They have security, even though it wasn't enough to stop me in my mouse form. It will be more complicated to deal with for people in their human forms, though."

"Do you know any kind of details about that security system?"

"Only bits and pieces. I'll tell you everything I know about that and the guards."

Sue nodded. "Good. It's going to take us a few days to put everything in place, but we'll manage."

Cedric frowned. "But we have to go right away." They had to before Archie got hurt. Rick wouldn't hesitate, not when he realized Cedric was never coming back. Cedric had to save his brother before anything happened to him. He wouldn't be able to forgive himself if he didn't. Archie was in this situation because of him. That meant that Cedric had to get him out of it.

Jonathan understood why Cedric wanted to go right away, but he also knew it wasn't possible. He wasn't looking forward to explaining that to Cedric, though. Cedric was terrified for his brother, and he would do anything to get him back, even if it was stupid. It was a small miracle that he hadn't found a way to try to rescue his brother by himself and that he hadn't gotten himself killed. Jonathan was relieved, but unfortunately, this wasn't over.

"We have to go right away," Cedric said.

Sue shook her head. "We can't. We have no idea what we would be walking into. I am *not* sacrificing my team members for that, no matter how much I want to help your brother."

"You only want to help because I know when Elroy is going to attack," Cedric snapped.

Jonathan had to keep things calm. He didn't want Cedric to make enemies, not in this room. He understood both sides of the situation, and he knew how hard it had to be for Cedric — and for Sue.

He crouched in front of his mate and took one of Cedric's hands. "We all understand why you want to go right away. We would if we could. But you said yourself that the place where Elroy lives is huge. It's a warehouse, right?"

Cedric looked like he didn't want to answer, but he nodded. "It is."

"And how many Beasts are usually there?"

"A lot. They're getting ready."

Jonathan's stomach churned. "That's why we can't just walk in. What's going to happen if the team gets caught? You know what Elroy would do better than anyone here, with the exception of Devon. We can't allow that to happen. We can't sacrifice any enforcer, especially not to when we're going to need all of them to protect Gillham."

"He's going to hurt my brother," Cedric said. There was so much pain in his voice that Jonathan wanted to say fuck it and go right away. He knew better than to do that, though. "I know. We're going to do everything we can, but I can't promise you will get him back. The chance we can do that will decrease if we don't prepare, though. I know you're worried and afraid, but this is our job. We know what we're doing, and we know how to do it well. Trust me. Trust us, Cedric."

Bran cleared his throat. "I'm sending a team in exploration right now. They'll check out the place, including security, and if possible, they'll see if Archie is actually there. You're not a hundred percent sure that's the case, right?"

Cedric shook his head. "They could have moved him since the last time I was there. I wouldn't be surprised if Rick did just that. He wants to hurt me. He knows that the best way to do that is through my brother."

"I understand. Let's hope he's still at the headquarters, then. I'll let you and Jonathan know as soon as we know anything. I promise."

Jonathan turned his attention to Bran. "Can we leave in the meantime?"

"Of course. I don't expect the two of you to hang around here until we find something. I'll call you if anything happens, but in the meantime, Cedric probably needs to rest."

Jonathan agreed. Even though Cedric had been sleeping a lot since yesterday, he still looked like he was about to fall on his face. "We'll be at my place. My phone will be on, so you can call anytime."

"Why are the two of you making decisions without even asking me?" Cedric groused.

It made Jonathan smile. There was the spitfire he was getting used to. "We're not. But Bran is right. It would be of no use to stay here, not when we can go to my apartment. We can head there, stop at the store to buy you clothes and whatever you want to eat, and settle down. You heard Bran. As soon as he knows anything, he'll let me know."

"I shouldn't go. I have to stay here to be ready as soon as we find out anything."

"Even if your brother *is* there, you won't go in with the team. You're not trained, and I can't allow anything to happen to you or to any of them. You have to stay back, which means that being at Jonathan's place won't change anything," Bran said.

"Which team are you sending?" Sue asked.

Bran turned to look at her. "Hopefully, yours. Everyone is in town, right?"

"They are. The few who had gone to visit family came back when I told them about Cedric being Jonathan's mate. They want to help."

"Good." Brandon looked at Jonathan. "What about you? Do you want to be part of this?"

Jonathan wanted to say yes. His team had never gone on a mission without him, not since he'd become a team member. He had to take care of Cedric, though. He couldn't leave him alone, and he didn't want to. "Unless Sue needs me, I'd rather stay here with Cedric, at least during the exploration. I can go with them when it's time to free Archie, though." He suspected Cedric would want him to.

"You can stay here for now," Bran agreed. "If needed, we can pull an enforcer from one of the teams in town. There are plenty of them we can use."

Jonathan didn't like the feeling of being replaced, but he knew Bran wasn't doing that. He also wasn't going to put the rest of the team in danger because they were missing one member, though.

Jonathan had thought Cedric would protest even more than he already had, but instead, he allowed Jonathan to lead him out. He looked lost, and it hurt Jonathan's heart to see it. He wanted to help. He wanted to give Cedric everything he wished for, but since that wasn't possible, he had to focus on something more practical.

"My apartment isn't far," he explained. "We can stop at the store to grab you more clothes, and if there's anything in particular you want to eat today, I can buy it for you."

Cedric shrugged. "I don't care."

Jonathan hoped it was the exhaustion and worry talking

and not something else. Since Cedric seemed to be in shock, Jonathan took charge. He was good at that, even though he wasn't his team's leader.

He drove them to the store. Cedric followed him around, looking both out of place and like he belonged. Jonathan could only imagine what it felt like to go back to a normal life after everything Cedric had gone through. He would do everything he could to help, but he wasn't sure there was much he could do. This was something Cedric would have to work on, but they didn't have time right now.

Jonathan grabbed several changes of clothes for Cedric, including pajamas and toiletries. Once that was done, he had to think about lunch and dinner. He had stuff for sandwiches in his fridge, and that would be fine for lunch. Dinner, on the other hand, was different. He wanted to impress Cedric. He knew it was ridiculous and that Cedric probably wouldn't care, not in the state he was in, but he wanted to show his mate that he could take care of him. He went for steak, along with a salad and baked potatoes. It was comfort food, and hopefully, it would help Cedric, even if only a bit.

They headed to Jonathan's apartment. He also had a room in the enforcers' building, and depending on how tired he was when he came back from a mission, he spent the night in either place. Now that he had Cedric, though, he knew he would surrender the room in the enforcers' building. He didn't want it anymore, not when Cedric would be waiting for him at home.

Hopefully.

"Here's the guest room," he explained as he showed Cedric the apartment. "There's a bathroom, so you don't have to use mine. I bought you some stuff for the shower. I'll be in the kitchen getting lunch ready. Do you need anything else?"

Cedric shook his head. "I'm not hungry."

"I know, but not eating isn't going to help your brother. Take a shower and try to relax. You can come out to the kitchen whenever you feel ready."

"Thank you," Cedric said.

Jonathan wished there was more he could do for him, but since there wasn't, he had to focus on what he *could* do, like feeding Cedric and making sure he was doing okay. Anything more than that would have to wait until Bran and Sue made their decisions.

Cedric felt horrible once Jonathan had left the room. He was touched by the way Jonathan was taking care of him, and he should have told Jonathan that. Instead, he'd only been able to focus on Archie and what was happening to him.

Jonathan understood, which made everything worse. Cedric wanted him to yell at him for ignoring him, or at the very least to push. Instead, Jonathan was doing everything he could to make Cedric happy, and Cedric wished he could be. He never would without Archie, though. He *had* to know what had happened to his brother, and he loathed that he had to wait.

He wanted to run back to Archie. He wanted to try to get him out of that place. Instead, he had to wait here for other people to make those decisions.

Having someone to take care of him felt good, but it was also confusing. Or maybe that was the mess of emotions Cedric was feeling. He was happy to have found Jonathan, but he felt guilty about it because he should be focusing on Archie. There was nothing he could do for his brother for now. Even if there was, he knew he wouldn't be up to it. He was still tired, hungry, and he felt weak. Rick had kept him that way on purpose so he wouldn't try to escape. That hadn't done Rick any good, but then, Cedric hadn't expected to be able to run away.

He hadn't been planning to, and when Devon had told him

to go, he'd obeyed on impulse. He should have thought better of it. If he had, Archie wouldn't be in the situation he was in right now, but then, neither would Cedric. If Cedric had stayed, both he and his brother would be stuck with Rick. There wouldn't be an enforcers' team getting ready to try to help Archie. Cedric wouldn't have found out when Elroy was planning to attack Gillham. So many things wouldn't have happened, and Cedric couldn't find it in himself to regret running away. He was terrified of what Rick was doing to Archie, but he knew that this was their only chance to make it out. Alone, they couldn't do anything. With an enforcers' team at their back, though, Archie would be free soon. Cedric had to believe that.

He had to do something. He couldn't let Jonathan do everything for him, no matter how much he wanted to snuggle in the bed and forget about everything that was happening around him. Instead of doing that, he showered, put on clean clothes, and headed out of the guest room.

He wasn't surprised Jonathan had shown him to a guest room instead of the master bedroom. He suspected Jonathan wanted him with him, but he would never push for something like that. Last night, he'd even slept on the floor. Cedric had offered to share the bed, but Jonathan had refused. He'd understood that Cedric felt vulnerable, and he'd wanted to make him feel better.

He had. Cedric couldn't believe Jonathan was his mate. He was such a caring man, so sweet and gentle. It was what Cedric needed after everything that had happened to him, and he wanted to give Jonathan more than he could. He wouldn't be able to until he was sure Archie was safe, but he knew Jonathan wouldn't resent him for that.

Jonathan was in the kitchen, and Cedric took a few moments to look at him. Jonathan moved easily, which made sense since this was his home. Cedric couldn't see what he was doing, since Jonathan's back was to him, but Jonathan had turned some music on, and he was gently swaying to the rhythm.

It was strange to see him in such an intimate situation. This probably wasn't something he did in front of anyone, and it touched Cedric that he felt comfortable enough to do it when he was in the apartment. He was conflicted. He felt guilty for wanting Jonathan when he should focus on Archie, but there was already enough guilt in his life.

He felt guilty about not telling Kameron what Elroy was planning right away. He felt guilty about putting Archie in Rick's path. He felt guilty about running away without his brother and not being able to help him.

He didn't want to feel guilty when it came to his mate. He didn't know what would happen between them, but he wanted to hope. Maybe, once Archie was safe and all of this was over, he and Archie could settle down in Gillham. Cedric hadn't seen a lot of it when Jonathan had driven through town, but the little he had told him that he and Archie could be happy here. Besides, it wasn't even about the town. It was about the people who lived here, and that included Jonathan.

Jonathan turned around, noticed Cedric, and smiled. "I thought you were going to take a nap before lunch."

Cedric shook his head. "I'm afraid that if I go to sleep now, I won't be able to rest tonight."

"Makes sense. Do you want to sit down? Lunch is about ready."

"Is there anything I can do to help?"

"Not really. Sit. I know you're still tired." Jonathan rubbed the back of his neck. "I wasn't sure what you liked, so I stayed simple. These are turkey, mayo, and tomato sandwiches. Just let me know if you want anything else, and I'll make sure you get it."

"They're perfect. Don't worry about it."

Jonathan smiled. "I doubt I'll ever be able to stop worrying when it comes to you. I want you to be happy and to feel safe."

"I do feel safe." It surprised Cedric, but he couldn't deny it.

He'd only met Jonathan yesterday, but it had been enough for him. They'd spent time together, and he *knew* Jonathan wouldn't hurt him. Jonathan was doing everything he could to make this situation easier on Cedric. He wasn't lying when he said that he wanted Cedric to be happy. Cedric wasn't sure it was possible, not without Archie by his side, but in the meantime, it felt good to be with Jonathan.

"I'm glad," Jonathan murmured.

"It doesn't make sense, but I don't want to fight this, not when I'm already fighting other battles."

"I understand. I'm happy you know that you can trust me. I won't let anything happen to you, and if I can, to your brother."

"I know. You're taking care of me. It's one of the reasons I trust you."

Jonathan nodded and gestured at the table. "Why don't you sit down? I'll get you your sandwich and something to drink. Is there anything in particular you want?"

"Whatever you have in the fridge." Cedric could too easily imagine Jonathan rushing out to get him what he wanted if he didn't have it already. He didn't want to be alone, though. It would be too easy for his thoughts to go back to Archie and what was happening to him, and he didn't want that to happen.

Obsessing over it wouldn't change anything, and it wouldn't help. It would only make Cedric feel worse and guiltier, and he didn't know if he could deal with that.

Instead of focusing on his brother, Cedric sat at the table. He listened to Jonathan grumble about how little stuff he had in the fridge and smiled. He wondered if this was what his life would be like once everything was over. Would he be living with Jonathan? Or would Jonathan want to take things slow? Would Cedric?

He didn't have answers to those questions, and he wouldn't get them until he had Archie back. In the meantime, though, it felt good not to be alone. It felt good to be taken care of, to feel *cherished*. Cedric knew that wasn't the case, not yet, not when he and Jonathan didn't know each other, but whatever was happening between them was a good step toward that, and he couldn't wait to see what would come next.

He couldn't wait to see what kind of life he would be able to build once he had both Archie and Jonathan in his life.

CHAPTER FIVE

Jonathan wasn't surprised to get a call the next day. He'd known his team and Bran wouldn't want to delay things, not with Elroy threatening the town. If they had to do this, they had to do it as soon as possible.

"We'll be there as soon as possible," he told Sue.

He couldn't see her expression, but he could hear the worry in her voice. "Good. We have a lot to talk about."

Jonathan wanted to ask if she'd changed her mind, but he didn't. He knew she wouldn't, but he also realized that getting Archie out of the Beasts' claws might not be as easy as they'd hoped.

They hung up, and Jonathan went to look for Cedric. He was in the guest room, hopefully still sleeping, and Jonathan didn't want to wake him up, especially not for this. He had to, though. Cedric would never forgive him if he didn't keep him up to speed with what was happening with the mission to rescue Archie. Besides, Sue and the others were waiting for them.

Jonathan knocked on the door. When he didn't get an answer, he gently pushed it open, relieved to see it was unlocked. He peered into the bedroom, but Cedric wasn't there. He didn't have time to get worried, though, because Cedric came out of the bathroom, wearing only a towel around his waist.

Jonathan knew he should look away, but he couldn't seem to. His gaze was fixed on Cedric's chest and the one drop of water rolling down it.

"You're staring," Cedric said.

Jonathan snapped his gaze away. Cedric sounded amused, but he didn't want to risk it. "I apologize."

"What are you apologizing for?"

"I shouldn't have walked into the bedroom."

"Why not? This is your home."

"And you're a guest." He would be much more if Jonathan had his way, but it was too soon, and Cedric was still focused on Archie, as was right.

"I'm not angry, Jonathan. Besides, it's not like you haven't already seen me mostly naked. You can look." Cedric hesitated. "We're mates. Eventually, you're going to see me naked."

Jonathan couldn't wait, but he didn't want to make Cedric uncomfortable. "Not if you don't want me to. Us being mates doesn't mean we have to be together, and I hope you know that."

Cedric was silent for a moment. Jonathan could hear him walk around the room, and he hoped Cedric was getting clothes. He wasn't sure whether Cedric was saying that he could watch him because he wanted it or because he felt he had to. The second option made Jonathan want to puke, and he hoped that wasn't the case.

He hadn't demanded anything from Cedric, and he didn't expect anything from him. They were mates, but Cedric had been through so much, and he was still going through a lot. Jonathan would feel like a dick if Cedric felt obligated to do or say something because of their bond.

"I do know that," Cedric finally said. "What *do* you want, though?"

"Honestly?"

Cedric chuckled. "I wouldn't ask if I didn't want an honest answer. Yes, honestly."

"I wish I could drag you into my arms and kiss you. Even

if that's everything you can ever give me, it will be good enough for me. I just want to be with you."

"But you haven't asked for it."

"Because I know now isn't the right moment. Your focus is on your brother, and I'm fine with that." Jonathan swallowed. He hadn't forgotten he had to tell Cedric about Sue's phone call. He'd been distracted, but Cedric would kick his ass if he didn't tell him. "Sue called."

"She did? Why?"

"Because the team went to the warehouse you told us to go to. They're back with information, and Sue thought it was a good idea to have us at the meeting."

Cedric was suddenly in front of Jonathan, and thankfully, he was dressed. "What are we waiting for?"

Jonathan couldn't help but smile. "Nothing. You did need to get dressed before we headed out, though."

Cedric shook his head, but he was smiling. "Let's go. I want to hear what they have to say."

So did Jonathan, so they didn't waste time. They climbed into Jonathan's truck and drove out to Gillham pack territory. Cedric kept bouncing his knee, but Jonathan didn't ask him to stop. He understood where the nervous energy came from, and he knew nothing would help. If this was a small relief for Cedric, he was welcome to it.

"What do you think they'll say?" Cedric asked as Jonathan drove into pack territory.

"I don't know. But they went there to gather information, so they'll no doubt talk about the security system, and of course, the number of Beasts present."

Cedric grimaced. "It's not going to be good. What if they decide it's not worth the risk?"

"You have to remember that whatever happens, even if no one else wants to go, I will."

"I don't understand why you'd want to do that. I know

we're mates, but we haven't even kissed yet. You don't know if we can work together as a couple, and as far as you know, I could leave as soon as I have Archie back. Why are you ready to sacrifice so much for me?"

"Because I like you. And yes, because you're my mate. I want to do this for you. I want to make you happy. My bear and I wouldn't feel right if we didn't at least try. It's more than that, though. No one should be abandoned, but especially not to the Beasts. Those guys are assholes, and I don't want your brother to have to stay with them one second longer. Hell, the time he already spent with them is too long. I might not want to do something stupid and go rescue him without having more information, but now I'll have it, and I can do something."

"You think your team won't want to help?"

"I think they'll do everything they can. You're my mate, and I'm their teammate. Unfortunately, we're enforcers, and we have to obey orders."

"What if your boss orders you to stay away from Archie?"

Jonathan sucked in a breath. He'd already thought about this, and he had an answer. He didn't like it, and he hoped it wouldn't come to that, but he'd made his decision. "I'll resign."

Cedric was silent until Jonathan parked the truck in front of Kameron's house. Then, he turned to face Jonathan.

Jonathan was surprised that he looked angry, and he wasn't sure what had prompted that emotion.

"You're ready to sacrifice everything you've worked for because of me?" Cedric asked.

"I am. I'm ready to sacrifice a lot for you, Cedric. I know you probably don't understand why, but it doesn't have to make sense. I want to help you. More than that, I want to help Archie. I understand why the council wouldn't want to send an enforcers' team to save him. It's dangerous, and they can't afford to lose an entire team, especially not now. They *can* afford to lose one enforcer, though. I won't leave your brother with the Beasts. Whatever we hear during the meeting, Archie will be safe eventually."

Jonathan had to convince himself of that. He didn't want to do it alone. He was used to working with his team, and it would be safer for him and for Archie. There had to be a lot of Beasts in that warehouse, and it was easy to imagine what would happen if one of them caught Jonathan.

But he would understand if his team couldn't go. It wouldn't stop him, though.

Cedric shook his head. "You can't sacrifice your life for me."

"I'm not. I'm planning on doing what's right. Whether or not I have to sacrifice my job for that doesn't depend on you. And before you say anything, I won't change my mind."

Cedric kept staring at Jonathan

Jonathan decided that they might as well head inside. The team was no doubt waiting for them, and they didn't have time to waste. He got out of the truck.

Cedric scrambled to follow him but said nothing.

That was concerning, but Jonathan didn't ask him what was going on in that head of his. He already knew the answer to that — Cedric was worried. He was being pulled apart from different directions, and he didn't know which way to go. He wanted Archie to be okay and for his brother to be saved, but he didn't want Jonathan to put his life and his career in danger for it.

He wouldn't have to make a choice, though. The only person who had to choose was Jonathan, and he already had.

"Wait," Cedric said.

Jonathan stopped moving, wondering what Cedric was going to say.

Cedric came to stand in front of him. Jonathan expected

him to berate him, or maybe to convince him not to do what he'd planned, but instead, he leaned closer and softly kissed Jonathan on the lips. "Thank you," he murmured.

Jonathan wasn't sure he could speak. He cleared his throat. "You have nothing to thank me for."

"I have a lot to thank you for, but now isn't the right moment to list all of them. I just wanted you to know that I *am* grateful, even when I don't sound like it." He stepped away. "Shall we go in?"

Jonathan wanted to kiss him again, but he knew better, so instead, he followed his mate inside Kameron's house as he shielded himself against whatever was about to happen.

Cedric didn't understand why Jonathan was ready to resign for him, but he wasn't going to fight it. He'd already protested, and he could tell he wouldn't change Jonathan's mind. Besides, he didn't really want to change it. He wanted someone to help Archie, and if no one else would, it was a relief to know that Jonathan would step in.

Still, Cedric was terrified for his mate. Cedric might lose his brother, and he didn't know if he could deal with losing his mate, too. He supposed he would find out eventually, which didn't help much, unfortunately.

They walked inside Kameron's house. Cedric was nervous, and part of him didn't want to go to the meeting. He didn't want to face how impossible the situation was. He wanted to keep believing that they could help Archie, but he knew it wouldn't work for much longer.

He reached out as he and Jonathan walked down the hallway to Kameron's office and linked their fingers together.

Jonathan jerked and looked at him.

Cedric didn't say anything, but he also didn't move his hand away. He hoped Jonathan didn't mind, and he was relieved when Jonathan squeezed and used their joined hands to drag him to the office faster. It made him smile, something he sorely needed.

Jonathan knocked on the door but opened it before anyone could answer.

Cedric could hear voices inside, so he doubted anyone would care. They stepped in, and Cedric blinked at the number of people who were present. The office was large, but with everyone there, it looked almost tiny.

"Who are these people?" he asked in a whisper, leaning closer to Jonathan.

"My team. Don't worry. They'll love you."

"That's not what I'm worried about."

Jonathan smiled. "I know it's not what you're worried about, but again, they won't care. Come on."

They'd all turned to look at Cedric and Jonathan when they'd entered, and Cedric felt slightly intimidated.

Jonathan started pointing at people. "You already know Sue. That's Davis, and that's Rose. There you have Janelle and Xander. Xander is our human."

A huge man grimaced, and Cedric blinked at him. He was even more intimidated now.

"Of course, you already know Nadha and Lorcan. Everyone, this is Cedric, my mate."

Cedric suspected they all wanted to come to him to say hello, especially Devon, who was standing near Lorcan, but instead, they limited themselves to nodding and smiling at him. He did the same, then turned his attention to the three people around the desk. Kameron was sitting in his chair, with Sue and Bran on the other side of the desk. Cedric held his breath, wondering what was about to happen.

Kameron smiled. "Cedric. Do you want to sit down?"

Cedric shook his head. "I just want to know what's going on."

"All right. Sue?"

She turned around to face Cedric. "The team just came back from the warehouse. The news isn't good. There are Nix blockers everywhere. Nadha had to shimmer us almost fifteen minutes away from the place. That probably wouldn't be too much of a problem if it weren't coupled with the rest. There are a lot of Beasts around, and by a lot, I mean more than fifty. As if that wasn't enough, the security system is incredible, with both alarms and guards. I don't know how you managed to sneak in, but the way I see it, it was a miracle."

Cedric had to swallow. "I did it in my mouse form. No matter how good the security system is, it can't do anything against a mouse."

"Well, none of us are mice shifters or anything that small. It's going to be a problem."

Cedric could feel the hope leaching from his body. "Does that mean you can't go?"

"Remember what I told you outside," Jonathan said. "Even if they can't, I will."

"That won't be necessary," Bran interrupted. "We *are* going. We have to be careful, though. It's extremely dangerous, both for the team and for Archie. It won't be easy to get him out of there."

Cedric had never quite thought about the dangers of Archie being caught while sneaking out, and he was horrified. "He could get hurt."

Bran's expression held a hint of pity that Cedric hated. "He could, yes. It's a possibility we have to consider. If you want your brother to be saved, we'll have to take some risks, both with our lives and his."

Cedric had to let go of Jonathan's hand so he could bury his face into his palms. He needed a moment, and it didn't help that everyone in the office was staring at him.

He rubbed his face, trying to think. He had to do more, but

what? He'd already tried to get to Archie, and it hadn't worked. On his own, he wouldn't be able to do anything. Rick wouldn't allow him to take Archie away. He wouldn't even allow him to *see* Archie. Cedric was ready to sacrifice a lot to save his brother, though, and it made him wonder.

Sneaking into the warehouse hadn't worked for him. Maybe something else would. Rick wanted him back. That was the only reason he still had Archie. What if Cedric gave himself up?

He dropped his hands, focused on his thoughts.

He didn't like the thought of giving himself up to Rick. He never wanted to see the man again, and he could too easily imagine what Rick would do to him if he went back. What if that was the only way to save his brother, though? Could Cedric ignore the opportunity he had to save his brother, even if it came to sacrificing his safety? He knew Jonathan would try to get to him. If he was lucky, Jonathan would manage to sneak in and save him, too.

But it would be dangerous, and something could happen to Jonathan. He could even die, and that wasn't something Cedric was willing to risk.

No. If he was going to sacrifice himself, he had to make it so Jonathan wouldn't be able to save him and that he wouldn't even try. He didn't know if that was possible, and he didn't have a lot of time to think about it, but he didn't want to dismiss it.

"Don't even think about it," Devon snapped.

Cedric blinked. He hadn't heard his friend come closer, and he didn't understand why Devon looked so angry. "What are you talking about?"

Devon pointed a finger at him. "I know what you're thinking. Trust me. I've gone through the same thoughts. I actually did it and left Gillham to give myself up to Elroy. You know how that went."

Cedric grimaced. "How did you know that was what I was thinking?"

Devon's expression shifted. He didn't look as angry now, but rather, tired and weary. "I wanted to save the town. I felt guilty because I knew that me being here would push Elroy to be even more cruel when it came to the people who live here. I hoped that by giving myself up, he would change his mind. I was wrong, and I knew I would be. I kept hoping, though." He reached out and took one of Cedric's hands. "Do you really think that Rick is going to let your brother go if you hand yourself over to him?"

"I can make him promise."

Devon snorted. "It wouldn't do you any good. I just told you what I did when I went back to Elroy, and it didn't work. If anything, it gave Elroy one more thing to taunt me with. He found it hilarious. We both know that even if you give yourself up, Rick won't let your brother go, and then you'll both be stuck with him. He'll keep on using Archie against you. Is that really what you want?"

Cedric sighed. "Of course not. What I want is for both Archie and myself to be safe."

"Then let us help you," Jonathan said.

Cedric was afraid to look at him. He didn't want Jonathan to be angry with him or disappointed. "I'm scared."

Jonathan took Cedric's free hand and squeezed. "I know. Your brother's life is in danger. We're going to do everything we can to save him, though. You don't have to sacrifice yourself to make that happen."

Cedric looked up. Everyone was still staring at him, and it made him uncomfortable. They all knew what he'd been thinking, and from their expressions, he was pretty sure none of them would allow him to even step toward the door at this point. "I don't know if there's anything else we can do," he said. "I know you want to help, and I know it's because I'm

holding a crucial piece of information from you. I would understand if you didn't want to sacrifice yourself for my
brother, though. On the other hand, he's my brother. If anyone has to sacrifice themselves, it's me."

Jonathan was panicking. He hadn't even realized that was
what Cedric was thinking until Devon had moved closer.
Cedric looked devastated, and Jonathan had felt the same
way once Devon had started talking and Cedric had admitted
what he was thinking about doing.

He couldn't. Jonathan wouldn't allow it.

"You don't have to sacrifice yourself," he told Cedric. He
didn't even care that everyone could hear what they were saying. He was making himself vulnerable, but it didn't matter.
All the people in this room, including Cedric, would have his
back.

"Why not?" Cedric asked.

It was a question he'd asked already, but he didn't seem to
believe the answer Jonathan had given him.

Jonathan gently pushed Devon away so he could take both
of Cedric's hands. Cedric wouldn't look at him, but it didn't
matter. Jonathan could still talk to him. "I know we just met,"
he started. "I already care about you, though, Cedric. I don't
want anything to happen to you or your brother. I know the
situation is complicated, but the only thing you'll achieve if
you give yourself up to Rick will be for him to have two hos-
tages instead of one. You really think I won't try to save you
if you go?"

Cedric grimaced and finally looked up. "You shouldn't. If
I sacrifice myself, it will be my decision."

"And it will be my decision to go after you. If you don't
want that to happen, you'll stay here and work with us instead of sneaking out like Devon did. Please."

Jonathan could see that Cedric wanted to say no. He thought this was the only way he could help his brother, and it made sense. If Rick wanted Cedric back, he was probably ready to promise anything to make that happen. Everyone in the room knew he wouldn't keep his promises, though.

"Just think about it," Jonathan said. "If you go, I'm coming after you. Nothing you can say would make me change my mind about that."

Cedric's shoulders slumped. "Fine. I won't rush into this, and I won't make stupid decisions. Not yet, anyway."

Jonathan supposed this was as good as he was going to get. "All right." He turned toward the rest of the team. "What now?"

"Now, we plan," Sue said. "Even though the situation is dire, it doesn't mean it's impossible. We're used to complicated missions, and this one isn't any different. Cedric, I know it's pointless to ask you not to worry, but we know what we're doing. Give us a day or two to plan everything and to make sure we know what we're headed into, and we'll go."

"What am I supposed to do in the meantime?" Cedric asked.

Sue looked from him to Jonathan. "Go home. There's nothing you can do to help. Jonathan, you can stay, but you already know what we're going to do. I think you should stay with Cedric, but it's your choice."

It was an easy choice to make. "I'll go home with Cedric. Let us know if anything happens and when you're thinking about going. I want to be there."

"Of course. Get some rest. With everything happening, none of us will be able to get a lot of it once all this starts."

She was right, and even though Jonathan wanted to stay and help his teammates, he knew his presence would be more useful to Cedric.

They were both silent as they headed back to Jonathan's

apartment. Jonathan hoped Cedric wasn't thinking about giving himself up again. He didn't know what he would do in that case. He would try to get Cedric to stay, but if Cedric did manage to sneak out—and it was possible, since he was a mouse shifter—Jonathan would go after him.

He hadn't been lying when he'd said that was exactly what he was planning to do. He wouldn't leave Cedric or Archie in Rick's hands. He wouldn't be able to live with himself if he did, and his mate didn't deserve to get hurt again. He'd already been through too much.

"I'm going to take a nap," Cedric said once they were in the apartment. He headed toward the guest room without looking back at Jonathan.

Jonathan sighed. He wanted to help Cedric, but he didn't know how or if he could. He'd already promised he would help Archie even if no one else would, and while he knew Cedric trusted him and believed he would, he could also tell it didn't help much with the worry.

Cedric was terrified. He was right to be, too. He knew the Beasts better than anyone except for Devon, and that meant he was aware of what they could and would do if he went back. The fact that he was willing to sacrifice himself for his brother was a stunning show of love, but it petrified Jonathan. Every time he thought about it, his stomach churned, and he felt like he was about to throw up.

He couldn't lose Cedric. They hadn't even kissed yet, beyond the quick contact earlier, but that would happen eventually, when the time was right. Even if it didn't, Jonathan didn't want Cedric to get hurt, or worse. Now that he'd met Cedric, he couldn't imagine a world without him in it, whether or not they were together. He still hoped they would be, of course, but it wasn't a necessity. What *was* a necessity was for Cedric to be safe.

Jonathan flopped onto the couch and stared at the ceiling.

He'd wanted to be here with Cedric if Cedric needed him, but now that Cedric was in the guest room, Jonathan wondered what the team was doing. They'd already been through several missions like this one, so he knew they were planning how to get around the security system and the guards. The fact that he would be there when they went in made him feel better, but he felt like he should be there with them, planning how to save Archie. Instead, he was sitting on his couch, alone. It would be worth it if Cedric needed anything from him, but so far, he seemed to want to be alone.

Jonathan sighed and rubbed his face. He was tired, and if he was honest, a nap didn't sound like a bad idea. Sue was right. With the attack looming on the horizon, they wouldn't have time to rest and nap once they started. Maybe he should take advantage of it.

He closed his eyes, but all thoughts of sleeping fled his mind when he heard the guest room door open. He listened to Cedric's footsteps come closer and waited. He didn't know what Cedric wanted, but he didn't want to push him into talking. Maybe he was just headed to the kitchen.

"Jonathan?" Cedric asked.

Jonathan opened his eyes and looked at him. "What is it?"

Cedric didn't look like he was sleepy. He looked tortured, though, and Jonathan's heart ached. He didn't want Cedric to feel that way. He didn't want him to think about sacrificing himself for his brother's sake. He was pretty sure Archie wouldn't want that, but Cedric didn't seem to care about anything but getting his brother back.

"I have to tell you something," Cedric said. He shuffled his feet and looked away.

Jonathan wondered why he appeared ashamed. "You can tell me anything. I hope you're not planning on sacrificing yourself again, but I'm willing to listen if you want to talk things out. I won't judge you."

Cedric chuckled darkly. "I don't know about that. The attack, the one I know about. Elroy is planning on attacking Gillham in two days."

The bottom of Jonathan's stomach dropped. "So soon?"

Cedric nodded. "I should have told you sooner. I was afraid for Archie, but it's wrong to keep your team focused on my brother when they need to prepare for the attack and to protect Gillham. I'm sorry."

Jonathan was angry, both at Cedric and Elroy. He knew Cedric had meant well, and he understood why he hadn't told anyone about the attack, but two days? Jonathan didn't know if the town would be ready to withstand the attack in such a short time, even though they were working on it already.

He sat up and reached for his phone in his pocket. "I have to call Bran and Kameron."

Cedric nodded. "I'm sorry."

Jonathan took a deep breath. "I know, and even though I *am* angry at you, I won't berate you for what you did." At least Cedric had told him what was going to happen before it did. That was what Jonathan had to focus on.

Cedric was pretty sure that was a lie. He could see Jonathan was angry at him, and he understood why. He didn't blame Jonathan, either.

He felt horrible. He should have told Jonathan, or even Kameron and Bran, as soon as he got to Gillham. He'd known the attack would happen in only three days, but instead of telling the people who needed to hear it, he'd kept it a secret. He'd been terrified they wouldn't help Archie, and now, he *knew* they wouldn't. They didn't have the time or the manpower to dedicate to rescuing his brother.

Sacrificing himself looked better and better as time passed.

It might be the only way for him to get his brother back. He knew Rick would probably lie, but maybe Cedric could find a way for him to let Archie go before he gave himself up. He couldn't count on the enforcers, not anymore, not when they had better things to focus on. He doubted he could count on Jonathan, either.

No matter what Jonathan had promised, he was angry with Cedric, and he wanted to protect Gillham. It was his job, and Cedric didn't want him to resign just because of him. He didn't want to have to choose between his brother's safety and his mate's or his, but he was going to have to.

"Kameron? Cedric needs to talk to you," Jonathan suddenly said.

Cedric blinked. He'd seen Jonathan take his phone out, but he hadn't realized they were on the phone already.

"Cedric?" Kameron asked.

Cedric swallowed. "I should have told you sooner, but Elroy is going to attack in two days, the day after tomorrow."

Kameron was silent. Cedric wondered if he was thinking of a way to kill him, or at the very least, hurt him. He wouldn't blame the alpha.

"Are you sure?" a different voice asked.

Cedric blinked at Jonathan, who mouthed, "Conference call."

Cedric nodded, even though Kameron and Bran couldn't see him. "I am. That's the information I was keeping from you. I'm sorry. I should have told you right away, because the attack is so soon. I was afraid for my brother, though."

"We understand," Kameron said.

Cedric didn't know how they could. He was angry with himself. Why wasn't everyone else?

"That changes things," Bran said. "We have to accelerate the timeline. Thanks for letting us know, Cedric."

"I'm sorry," Cedric repeated. He was pretty sure that no matter how many times he told them he was sorry, it wouldn't make him feel less guilty. He shouldn't, not after what he'd done.

"That could be a good thing," Kameron said.

Cedric frowned. "What are you talking about?"

"Your brother. We've known for a while that the Beasts were going to attack, so we're fairly ready to face them. We just have to accelerate the timeline, just like Bran said. It could be good when it comes to Archie, though. If the Beasts are here in Gillham, they won't be at the warehouse. Even if Rick leaves one or two behind, the warehouse will be empty."

Cedric blinked. "What are you saying?"

"That this would be the perfect moment to get to your brother. You said Rick works closely with Elroy. That means he's going to be in Gillham, right?"

"No doubt about it."

"So you and Jonathan would only have to face a few guards."

It wouldn't work. "I can't keep Jonathan away from Gillham. He needs to protect the town and the pack. It's his job."

"I'm going with you," Jonathan said. His tone was hard, but Cedric knew it was only because he was worried.

Jonathan cared, so much more than Cedric could understand. Or maybe he could. After all, he cared about Jonathan, too. If he didn't, he wouldn't have a problem with Jonathan going with him to get Archie. He wouldn't have a problem with Jonathan proposing he sacrifice himself for Archie and Cedric's sake.

"Jonathan is right," Bran said. "While I don't like the thought of one of my teams missing a member, I know I can pull someone from another team in another city or even another country. It won't be the same, but it won't be a problem, either. I could probably send someone with the two of you, too."

"I think it's better if only the two of us go," Jonathan said.

There was a tone of authority in his voice, and Cedric wondered if eventually he would become a team leader. He could see it easily, even though he wasn't sure he liked the thought. It would put Jonathan in even more danger, although considering the situation he'd put Jonathan in, it wasn't his place to point that out.

"I agree," Bran said. "Cedric, do you know what Elroy is going to do? Where he's going to attack, how many people he'll have with him?"

"I don't know. I heard the date when he was talking with Rick, and I know that his final target is the pack, Kameron especially. I doubt they're going to attack the humans, not if they stay out of the way. You should try to find a way to keep people inside their homes." There was so much to do that Cedric wanted to cry. Why had he kept this secret?

He hadn't trusted the pack, Jonathan, or anyone else, but they'd welcomed him. They'd been ready to help him, and what had he done to thank them? Kept a secret one day too many.

"Focus on your brother. We have everything in hand. Jonathan, keep me up to date. Even though there's a lot going on, I want to know what's happening with you. The two of you should prepare, too. Even though you'll probably only face a few guards, you'll still have to be careful, and we don't know if Rick expects this to happen. It might be a trap. Call Sue to get all the information she and the others have."

That made Cedric feel even worse.

"I'll call you as soon as Cedric and I decide what to do," Jonathan agreed. "You focus on Gillham and the pack. We'll be fine."

"I hope *everyone* will be fine. Talk to you soon," Kameron said.

Cedric didn't know if they'd hung up, but he thought they had. He wasn't sure he could face Jonathan, not after everything that had been said. He didn't want to see his mate disappointed, even though Jonathan would be in his right to be. Even Cedric was disappointed in himself.

"Cedric?" Jonathan asked as he got up from the couch and moved closer.

Cedric screwed his eyes shut and refused to look at his mate. "I'll understand if you never want to see me again. I know you feel obligated to help me with Archie, but you don't have to. If the warehouse is going to be empty like we think, I can probably get Archie on my own."

"Why do you think I wouldn't want to help you?"

"I don't understand why you would *want* to help me after what I did. I knew what was going to happen and that it was going to happen soon, but I still kept it a secret. I shouldn't have."

Cedric jerked when something touched his cheek, but it was only Jonathan. Cedric couldn't do anything but stare at his mate as he gently cupped one of Cedric's cheeks.

"I won't deny I was angry," Jonathan said. "I still am, but only slightly. This wasn't your fault. Elroy was always planning to attack, and our response has only been delayed by one day. Besides, we already knew about this. We're more than ready to face him. Having a two-day notice is more than we expected to have. If it weren't for you, we wouldn't know about it, and we would have to wait to react when Elroy gets here. This way, both the town and the pack have time to get ready and be prepared."

"I can't believe you see the good in this situation."

Jonathan chuckled. "How could I not? I still understand why you kept a secret, and I don't blame you for it. No one does."

Cedric had a hard time believing that. "What now?"

"Now, we get ready. We have two days to focus on what we're going to do to get to your brother. We should use both those days."

Cedric agreed, but he had something else in mind. "I want us to bond."

Jonathan's eyes widened. "What?"

"You heard me. You can say no if you don't want to, and I won't push or ask why. I do want it, though."

"Why?"

Cedric swallowed and looked away. "Because you're the only one who cares. Because I want to feel loved. I want to feel cherished." He might lose all of that in two days, and he wouldn't be able to forgive himself if he didn't give Jonathan at least this. Besides, he wanted to give it to himself, too.

Jonathan stared at him for a moment. Cedric expected him to say no, and he was both elated and relieved when Jonathan nodded. "All right. We can bond."

Cedric breathed easier, but Jonathan wasn't done.

"Do you want to do it here?" he asked.

Cedric frowned. "I thought the bedroom would be better, actually."

Jonathan hesitated. "All right. I just want you to know I don't expect you to do anything. We can limit ourselves to bonding and think about the rest later, when you feel up to it."

"The rest?" Cedric suspected he knew what Jonathan was thinking about, but he wanted to be sure.

To his surprise, Jonathan's cheeks turned pink. "You know. Sex. You didn't tell me what Rick did to you exactly, but I can imagine, which is why I want you to know I'm fine with just bonding. I don't want you to feel obligated or to do something you're not ready for."

Cedric beamed. He was pretty sure Jonathan thought he was nuts, but he didn't care. He moved toward his mate and reached up, pulling him closer so he could kiss him. "Thank you," he murmured against Jonathan's lips.

"I'm confused."

Cedric stepped back, but he didn't let go of his mate. He took Jonathan's hand and linked their fingers together. "I'm touched that you're thinking about that. I won't lie and tell you that Rick didn't force me into his bed, but while it was horrible, it has nothing to do with you. I want this, Jonathan. I promise."

Jonathan stared at Cedric. "All right. But if there's anything wrong, please, tell me."

Cedric nodded. He already knew nothing would be wrong. He was with his mate, after all.

He pulled Jonathan toward Jonathan's bedroom. He was relieved when Jonathan didn't protest again, and even more so when they reached the bedroom. It was a bit messy, but Cedric didn't care. The only thing he cared about was Jonathan and being with him.

Neither of them knew what would happen next. The Beasts would attack Gillham, and Jonathan and Cedric would try to save Archie. But even if something happened to them, they would always have this moment.

Cedric turned around to face Jonathan. Jonathan reached for him, and they kissed again. Jonathan's hands drifted over Cedric's body, still hesitant, but Cedric would have none of that. He reached for his own t-shirt and pulled it up, eager to get naked with his mate. Jonathan had already seen him almost entirely bare, but never in these circumstances, and Cedric couldn't wait.

Jonathan chuckled, probably at how eager Cedric was, but Cedric didn't care. He *was* eager to make love with Jonathan and to bond with him. Who would blame him for that? Certainly not Jonathan, who was getting rid of his own clothes.

He'd thrown his t-shirt to the floor, and Cedric leaned forward, sticking his tongue out and lapping at Jonathan's nipple. Jonathan shuddered, making Cedric smile.

It had been a long time since he'd done this because he wanted to, and he couldn't wait. He still had nightmares about Rick, and he knew that making love with Jonathan wouldn't make them magically disappear or that bonding with his mate wouldn't erase the trauma he'd come through. He still wanted to do it, though. He had to.

He wanted to know how Jonathan felt. He wanted to be with him, always. He wanted to have something for himself, to start building a life. Neither of them knew what would happen the day of the attack, but Cedric could begin building the future. It would give him one more reason to be careful and make it out of the attack alive.

He pressed his lips along Jonathan's chest, eager to taste more of his mate. Jonathan was a caretaker, though, so Cedric wasn't surprised when he gently pushed him away. He continued pushing until the back of Cedric's legs hit the mattress. Then, with a grin, he gave Cedric one last push.

Cedric tumbled onto the bed. He couldn't stop smiling, and he didn't want to. He watched as Jonathan crouched in front of him, taking his shoes off, then his socks. Then came time for Cedric's jeans.

Cedric's mouth went dry as Jonathan moved above him. Looking Cedric in the eyes, he kissed Cedric's chest and went down. His lips were light, but they branded Cedric as his. Jonathan didn't stop, continuing his path to Cedric's groin. Once he got to the jeans, he paused, kissing the patch of skin just above the waist. He raised his hands, unbuttoned the jeans, then gently pushed them down.

Cedric wiggled, trying to help, but Jonathan didn't need his help. He looked like he knew what he was doing, and while it was strange to relax and let him do everything, Cedric didn't have anything against it. If anything, he wanted more of it. He wanted Jonathan to take care of him. He wanted to feel cherished, loved, and Jonathan was giving him that.

Once Cedric was naked, Jonathan stood above him, watching him. Cedric was hard, but he wasn't ashamed. Jonathan already knew what Cedric wanted, so there was no way he was surprised about that.

Cedric reached down and wrapped his fingers around his cock. Jonathan grumbled and arched a brow at him, as if asking what he was waiting for. That was precisely what Cedric was wondering, so he moved his hand up and down, teasing Jonathan and hoping to make him go faster. He needed his mate, and he needed him now.

Jonathan chuckled and finally went to work on his own clothes. Luckily for Cedric, he was already bare-chested, so it didn't take that long for him to be entirely naked. Once he was, Cedric couldn't help but stare.

Jonathan was tall, and his shoulders were wide. It would feel so good to be snuggled against him, and so safe. Cedric couldn't wait to see what the aftermath of this would be like, what Jonathan would feel, what he would say. First they had to go through this, though, and it would be far from a hardship.

Jonathan was hard, too. The patch of hair that led down to his cock made Cedric's mouth water. He sat up, but he wasn't surprised when Jonathan shook his head.

"Stay where you are. I'll take care of you," Jonathan declared.

Cedric huffed, but he was more than happy to obey. He leaned back against the pillows, still touching himself, and watched his mate move around the bed. He opened the nightstand drawer and took out some lube, and Cedric groaned.

"We're going to need that," he said.

"I know. Spread your legs."

Cedric obeyed once again. He wasn't surprised when Jonathan spread himself onto the mattress between his legs. He was mouth to cock with Cedric, and Cedric's cock twitched. For whatever reason, it made Jonathan smile. Cedric wanted to tell him to make a move, but he kept his mouth shut, even though it was difficult.

Jonathan opened the lube and slicked his fingers. Cedric held his breath, knowing what was about to come. The tip of Jonathan's fingers touched his hole, but at the same time, Jonathan swallowed Cedric's cock. Cedric's back arched without him even thinking about it. He hadn't expected this, but he probably should have, knowing Jonathan.

God, how he'd missed blowjobs. The warmth, the slickness, the suction. All of that was heaven, and he'd thought he would never have it again. It was a good distraction, and when he realized Jonathan's finger was already inside him, he didn't even care. He wanted more. He needed more, and he knew Jonathan would deliver.

He raised his legs and bent his knees, planting his feet onto the mattress. He wanted to tell Jonathan to hurry up, but he knew it wouldn't work. Jonathan would do this at his pace, not one second sooner.

That was fine with Cedric, although he wondered if one could die from having blue balls. He hoped not. He wanted to do this many more times.

"You know you don't have to coddle me, right?" Cedric asked. He sounded out of breath.

There was a loud pop as Jonathan let go of Cedric's cock. "I'm not coddling you. I'm prepping you. I'm giving you pleasure. Isn't that what you wanted?"

"It is. I want you inside me, though. Please." Cedric knew that having Jonathan make love to him wouldn't make him forget every time Rick had done this to him, but he wanted to replace those memories. He wanted to make love, and he wanted to do it with Jonathan.

Just like he'd thought, though, Jonathan took his time. He

kissed Cedric's stomach, his thighs, his cock. He sucked and licked him until Cedric was quivering under him. Cedric wanted to scream, but he felt out of breath, so he wasn't sure he could if he tried. His legs trembled, and his fingers were buried in Jonathan's hair. Jonathan had let Cedric move him, though, and he was still focused on prepping him. Cedric wasn't even sure how many of Jonathan's fingers were inside him right now, but he desperately needed Jonathan to replace them with his cock.

"I'm ready," he panted.

"Are you sure?" There was a hint of hesitation and fear in Jonathan's expression.

Cedric understood it, but he wanted Jonathan to forget all about that. He opened his arms, hoping it would be enough to answer what Jonathan was asking.

Jonathan moved slowly. He removed his fingers from Cedric's body, then sat up on his knees. "Maybe you could turn around."

Cedric blinked. "I can if you want me to, but how are we going to bond that way?"

To Cedric's surprise, Jonathan lowered himself on top of Cedric. Cedric expected him to fuck him, but instead, Jonathan tilted his head to the side. "Bite me now. Unless you really want us to bite each other at the same time. I don't. However we do this, the important thing is that we do it."

Cedric agreed, so Jonathan didn't have to ask him twice. He bit into the offered flesh, his mouth filling with blood once he started sucking. He wasn't sure how much he had to drink, but he didn't want not to get enough, so he made sure he swallowed several mouthfuls. Once he was done, he licked the bite closed, feeling smug at the sight of it on Jonathan's throat.

"Ready?" Jonathan asked.

Cedric looked at him to make sure he wasn't in pain, but

Jonathan was smiling softly. When Cedric nodded, he got back onto his knees, giving Cedric space to move around. Cedric got to his hands and knees. It wasn't a position Rick had used a lot. He'd wanted to see the pain and hatred in Cedric's eyes when he hurt him. Cedric didn't want to think about Rick now, though. He wanted to focus on his mate and no one else.

He lowered himself on his elbows and looked back. Jonathan looked magnificent behind him. He was holding his cock, aiming it at Cedric's hole, and Cedric tensed. He knew he shouldn't, though, so he forced himself to relax. He breathed in and out, especially when Jonathan breached him.

It was painful, but nothing like what Rick had done. It was so easy to focus on Jonathan, on the reason they were doing this, and on the emotions they shared. Jonathan would never hurt Cedric and knowing that helped Cedric relax even more.

"All right?" Jonathan asked when he bottomed out.

Cedric had to press his forehead against his arms because he knew he wouldn't be able to keep on looking at his mate once Jonathan started fucking him. "Perfect. Come on."

Jonathan huffed a laugh. "I should have known you'd be demanding in bed."

"You haven't seen anything yet. Now get on with it. I'm waiting for my orgasm."

This time, Jonathan was the one who obeyed. He gripped Cedric's hips and slammed into him. Cedric groaned, wanting more, but he didn't have to ask for it. Jonathan delivered, apparently reading his thoughts.

Jonathan fucked Cedric the way Cedric wanted him to. He was strong, but not forceful. It was clear that if Cedric wanted him to, he would stop in an instant, and that was reassuring. It also meant that Cedric could focus on his pleasure.

He reached for his cock, but Jonathan beat him to it. He swatted Cedric's hand away and grabbed Cedric's cock, and it felt better than anything Cedric could have done. Jonathan's hand was bigger, stronger, and seemed callused. The sensation was maddening, and Cedric found himself biting his arm to stop from crying out. Then he remembered that no one would care if he was screaming out. There was no one else in the apartment.

He let go. He couldn't remember the last time he'd felt such pleasure. Jonathan was stimulating his entire body, or at least, that was what it felt like, until Jonathan moved his hand to Cedric's chest. Cedric was about to protest when Jonathan helped him rise to his knees. The penetration wasn't as deep now, but Jonathan made up for it by grabbing Cedric's cock again, then, by biting him.

The flash of pain was nothing against the pleasure that flooded Cedric as soon as it was gone. It was too much, too many sensations, and he couldn't have stopped himself from coming even if he wanted to. He didn't, though. He wanted Jonathan to know how much he loved this.

He came as Jonathan drank down his blood, linking them together. He'd thought he was overwhelmed before, but it became even worse once the bond snapped into place. He could feel Jonathan's pleasure as strongly as he could feel his own, and he was pretty sure he came a second time just then.

It was perfect, though. Even though he was exhausted, he could feel the exact moment in which Jonathan came inside of him. It was a strange sensation, Jonathan pulsing inside his body while also pulsing inside his mind.

They stayed in that position for a few moments, frozen. Cedric's legs wouldn't hold him up for long, though, and his hips folded up on him. Jonathan laughed and slowly lowered them to the mattress. He was still inside of Cedric, and from the feel of it, he wasn't planning on leaving his body anytime soon.

"Still okay?" Jonathan asked, stroking a hand down

Cedric's side.

Cedric huffed and sighed in pleasure. "More than okay. We should do this more often."

Jonathan laughed again and kissed Cedric's shoulder. "I'm at your disposal."

It was hard to believe, but he was right. He would always be there for Cedric, just like Cedric would always be there for him.

Chapter Six

Jonathan looked around. Everyone was ready for a fight, including him, even though he wouldn't be in Gillham when it happened. He would have his own fight to deal with, though, and hopefully, he'd be back soon so he could help defend the pack.

He didn't want Cedric to come with him. He was terrified at the thought of Cedric being hurt, but he wasn't sure he would feel better if Cedric stayed in Gillham. The place was going to be crawling with Beasts in only a few hours, probably sooner.

Jonathan knew that if Cedric wasn't with him, he wouldn't be able to focus on anything else. He needed to see that Cedric was safe, even though he suspected it would distract him. Cedric didn't know how to fight. He was strong, and he was a fighter, but not the physical kind. There was no way Jonathan was leaving him behind, though. Cedric wouldn't allow him to, and he might need help.

"I'm nervous," Cedric murmured.

He was wearing an enforcer's uniform. It looked strange on him, like it didn't belong, and Jonathan hoped Cedric wasn't going to get any ideas. Jonathan would support him whatever he wanted to do, but he really hoped Cedric didn't want to become an enforcer. "It's normal. I'm nervous, too. Everyone is always nervous and a bit afraid before a mission."

Cedric turned wide eyes to Jonathan. "You're scared?"

Jonathan couldn't help but smile. "I am. I think it's a good thing, though."

"How can fear be a good thing?"

"When you're not afraid, you tend to be distracted, and even worse, overconfident. I don't want to underestimate the people left at the warehouse or the security system. I know the Beasts will be focused on Gillham, but the last thing we need is for any of them to come back because they find out we're there."

Cedric slowly nodded. "I see. Well, I'm not sure it helps much, because I'm still scared, but I guess there's nothing I can do about it."

Jonathan cupped the back of Cedric's neck and pulled him closer until he could place a kiss on top of his head. "You'll be fine. I'll make sure of it." Even if it was the last thing he did.

He was willing to sacrifice himself for Cedric and his brother. He hoped it wouldn't come to that, but if it did, he wouldn't regret it. He wanted Cedric to live. He wanted his mate to be happy, to have everything he'd ever wanted in life. If something happened to him, Cedric would be hurt, especially since they'd bonded, but he would go on. He wouldn't be alone anymore, and Jonathan found peace in that thought.

Bran cleared his throat, and everyone in the room turned to look at him. He wore a uniform, too, and Jonathan knew he would fight, just like every single enforcer, pack security member, and probably a lot of other people. They were ready to face the Beasts, even though they weren't looking forward to it. They would keep Gillham safe because it was their job, but more importantly because Gillham was their home.

"I just got word that several Beasts were sighted at the edge of town."

Jonathan swore, and he wasn't the only one. They'd known this would happen, but now it was reality. There was no going back.

"Everyone, you know what to do," Bran continued. "Get to your spot. Jonathan and Cedric, Nadha will shimmer you to

106

where you have to go. She'll keep her phone on her, so if you need help, let her know."

Jonathan nodded. It was what they'd agreed on, but he knew that if he could avoid it, he wouldn't call Nadha. He couldn't afford to distract her, not when she would be fighting in Gillham.

He jerked away when he felt something touch his hand, but when he looked to the side, he realized it was Cedric, who took Jonathan's hand and squeezed after linking their fingers together. Jonathan wasn't used to this, and he was terrified at the thought of his mate being hurt.

But Cedric had more reasons to be afraid. They were going to try to save his brother, but they might fail. He'd also kept the secret that Elroy was coming to Gillham today, and even though he'd confessed only one day later, he felt guilty. No one had held it against him, but it would take some time for him to realize that.

For that to happen, he would have to come back to Gillham, and Jonathan would make sure he did. He also would make sure Archie had a good chance at life. He didn't deserve everything he'd gone through, and neither did Cedric. If Jonathan could do anything to help them, he would.

Bran strode toward them, Nadha behind him. Everyone else in the room was leaving, ready to fight. Bran stopped in front of Jonathan, staring at him. "Let us know if you need anything, and I mean that."

"I will."

Bran arched a brow, obviously knowing Jonathan better than Jonathan had expected him to. "It's an order. Even though I'm not your team leader, I *am* your boss. If you need anything, call Nadha, or even me. I'll send someone to you."

"I will. I hope I won't need it, though."

"With the number of Beasts coming to Gillham, I doubt you will. Still, the security system could be more advanced than we think. They also could have left more guards than we expect. Be careful, both of you, and come back to Gillham in one piece."

Jonathan squeezed Cedric's hand as he nodded. "I can't promise that, but I'll do my best."

"I suppose that's all we can hope for. Good luck."

They would need it, and so would Gillham and everyone who would fight for it.

Jonathan turned his attention to Nadha. She looked worried, but then, they all did. "We're ready when you are," he told her.

Nadha held her hand out, and Jonathan took it. Cedric didn't have to, since they were still holding hands, but he nodded. She shimmered them away. Jonathan left a piece of his heart in Gillham, but he had to focus on the situation he was in now.

Nadha let go of his hand once they'd arrived and looked at him. "If something happens to you, I'll hurt you," she promised.

Jonathan grinned. "Even if I'm already hurt?"

"That's why you better be careful."

"You, too. I'll call you as soon as we're done here."

"I'll be waiting."

"Keep everyone safe for me, will you?"

She grimaced. "I'll try, but I can't make promises. You know how the team is."

Jonathan did, which was why he wished he could be with them. They knew what they were doing, though, and so did he. Still, it was the first mission they weren't working together since Jonathan had become part of the team, and it was going to be strange. Jonathan realized that was one of the reasons he was so anxious about it. He wanted to be in two places at once, and it wasn't possible.

Nadha shimmered away, and Jonathan stared at the spot

in which she'd been for a few seconds. Then he turned to Cedric. "Ready?"

Cedric nodded. His expression hardened, and even though Jonathan could feel fear trickling through their bond, he didn't ask about it. They were both afraid, and there was no shame in that.

They walked until they reached the warehouse. It took about ten minutes, and Jonathan was hypervigilant the entire time. Every time he heard a noise, he jumped, but they got there without trouble. Once they were in front of the warehouse, they looked at each other again. "I still don't like this," Jonathan said.

"I don't like it either, but it's the best way for you to get inside."

"What if something happens to you?" They'd gone over this already, but Jonathan still hated the fact that Cedric was going to shift and sneak inside. It was one of the reasons he wished Cedric had stayed back.

"Then something happens to me. Nothing will, though." Cedric reached for Jonathan, and Jonathan gathered him into his arms. They didn't kiss. Instead, they pressed their foreheads together.

They hadn't been together long, just a few days, but it was enough for Jonathan to know that if something happened to Cedric, his life would be destroyed. Cedric was already a central part of it, and Jonathan didn't even want to think about the possibility that he wouldn't come out of the warehouse.

Cedric took a deep breath. "I'll stick to the plan. I promise. I'll go in, look around to see how many people are inside, and open a door for you to come in. It won't be long, only ten minutes at the most, I promise."

"You can't go through the entire warehouse in ten minutes."

"I can't, but I know where the guards will be if there are

any. Trust me."

"I do trust you." But Jonathan didn't trust the Beasts, and that was who they were going to have to face.

Sneaking inside the warehouse was easy. Cedric had done it several times, and this time was even easier because the warehouse was basically empty.

He knew he had to be careful. Even though no one was outside, there were no doubt at least a few guards still around. That was why he was entering first. Jonathan had wanted to say no, but Cedric had insisted that as a mouse, he could sneak around and count the guards, as well as hopefully turn off the security system. Cedric wasn't happy about it, either. He was terrified, and he knew what would happen to him if anyone found him. He wasn't going to put his mate or his brother in more danger than they already were, though. If this was something he could do, he would do it.

Hopefully, it wouldn't end with him in the cell next to his brother's. He wanted to go home with Jonathan. He wanted to show Archie that they could have another life. Cedric had barely started to explore it as it was, but he was ready for it. As soon as this place was behind them, and of course, as soon as Gillham was safe, he was going to do everything he had wanted to do during the time he'd spent in Rick's hands. He was free, and his brother would be, too.

He couldn't think of any other outcome.

He snuck inside the warehouse through the same opening he'd used in the past. The place was eerily silent, and he wasn't used to it. He suspected that someone would hear him, even though he was in his mouse form, so he had to be incredibly careful. He didn't want to ruin the mission by making too much noise. The guards might not think anything about it, since Cedric wasn't the only mouse around, but still. He couldn't risk getting shot at, and that was what the Beasts did to mice. Rick had taken much pleasure in demonstrating this to Cedric in the past.

But Cedric couldn't think about Rick right now. He had to focus on finding Archie, counting the guards, and letting Jonathan in. Unfortunately, the finding Archie bit would have to come last.

Cedric rushed around, peeking into the rooms as he passed. They were empty, which was good, but he still counted four guards. There were probably more, so Cedric continued moving around. He heard some of them talking, and they sounded excited. Cedric's stomach churned at the thought that they were excited about hurting people. He'd always known the Beasts were cruel, so he wasn't surprised, but he couldn't understand how a human being could think that way.

Who cared who was a human and who was a shifter? It didn't make a difference. Cedric wouldn't have cared if Jonathan had been human, or even himself. It was hard to imagine life without his mouse half, but he supposed he wouldn't even have known the difference if you'd been born human. He hadn't been, though, and he was glad right now, because if he had, he wouldn't be taking advantage of how small he could become.

"Put him downstairs," one of the guards said as he talked on the phone.

Cedric frowned. Who were they supposed to put downstairs? Archie? But his cell was already downstairs. So had Cedric's been, although Rick had taken pleasure in parading him through the warehouse to his bedroom. Everyone had known why and what he was going to do to Cedric once they got there, but no one had ever tried to protect Cedric. If anything, it was the opposite. They'd found it funny, and Cedric had soon learned not to fight it.

One of the doors that led outside slammed open. Cedric jumped and rushed under a table, hoping no one would see him. It wasn't the best hiding place, but it didn't seem to matter, because all the guards were focused on what was happening at the door. A man walked in, pushing his phone into his pocket, and he wasn't alone. There was another guard behind him, and that one was pushing Jonathan.

Cedric had to breathe deeply. His vision was closing in around him, but now, both Archie and Jonathan needed him.

"Who's your little friend?" one of the Beasts asked.

Cedric was pretty sure his name was Hank or something like that. He'd never bothered learning their names, but he did remember some of them.

"Well, he's wearing an enforcer's uniform, so you can bet he comes from Gillham," the Beast who'd been pushing Jonathan inside said.

Jonathan looked stoic. He didn't look around, didn't try to find Cedric. He didn't even betray the fact that he wasn't alone.

"He can go right downstairs. We have to find out why he's here. Elroy will have our asses otherwise."

"Can I play with him?" one of the Beasts asked, and Cedric was sure of his name this time.

Of the Beasts, Bill was probably the worst after Rick. He took pleasure in hurting people, and Cedric could see how happy he was about getting his hands on Jonathan.

Cedric had to do something. What, though? He was only a mouse shifter. He wasn't an enforcer or a fighter. Yet he was the only way out of this for Jonathan and Archie.

If Cedric managed to find a phone, he could probably call the enforcers, but how was he supposed to do that? Now that the guards knew that Jonathan was there, they were going to be extra careful.

Cedric hesitated. He had to do *something*. He couldn't leave his mate in the hands of the Beasts.

As much as he wanted to stay there and watch what happened, he knew they were going downstairs, so he had to get there first. Archie was in the basement, too, and maybe if Cedric managed to sneak into his cell, they could come up with a plan together. It probably wasn't the best idea, but so far, it was the only one Cedric had.

He rushed downstairs as quickly as his tiny mouse form would allow him to. He'd spent so much time as a mouse that he was an expert at maneuvering the spaces, so it took him no time to get to Archie's cell. Once he was there, though, Cedric wasn't sure how to sneak in. He looked at the small opening at the top of the metal door. If he shifted, he would be able to see Archie, but he would also risk being seen. That was the only way he could go in, though.

He looked down the hallway, and while he could hear voices, he couldn't see anyone yet. He was going to have to risk it.

He shifted back into his human form, hooked his fingers around the bars, and shifted again. He almost tipped back in the hallway instead of into the cell, and he had to push his body through the bars. Once he had, though, it was a freefall.

He shifted as he fell, afraid to hurt his mouse form if he didn't. Luckily for him, as a human, the fall wasn't a big one, even though he landed on his ass.

"Well, I can't say I ever wanted to see you naked," Archie said. There was humor in his voice, even though when Cedric looked at him, he was chained to the wall.

Archie was pale and had too-long hair and dark-shadows under his eyes. He looked like he hadn't eaten a good meal in a while, and Cedric's heart squeezed painfully. "You should be used to it. We're shifters," he said.

"You might be right, but we haven't seen each other in a while. What are you doing here?" Archie peered at the door.

"What's going on? I heard a lot of noise earlier, then nothing. It's eerie."

A door slammed open in the distance, and they both held their breath. Cedric knew his eyes were wide, and he had to explain what was going on to Archie, but he didn't know how.

He moved closer so that he could whisper to his brother. "The Beasts are attacking Gillham. That's what you heard. The warehouse is almost empty."

"Rick would never leave the place empty."

"There are several guards, and they captured my mate."

Archie sucked in a breath. "Your mate?"

"I'll tell you all about it, but we have to save Jonathan first."

"I'm chained to the wall, but see that key over there?" Archie asked, tilting his chin toward the metal door.

Cedric looked at it, his gaze stopping on a key hanging on the wall next to it. "What's it for?"

"My shackles. Rick left it there to torture me. But even if you take it and open the shackles, we can't go. You said there are guards."

"We have to look for Jonathan. You can stay with me and help, or you can leave the warehouse and I can look for him on my own. I can't leave him behind, though."

"Of course not. He's your mate. And I'm not going anywhere without you. I don't know if I can do this, though."

"I don't know if I can do it, either, but I'm not allowing anyone to make me a prisoner ever again. I don't care if I have to die. I don't want you to sacrifice yourself, though. You should probably go."

Archie stared at Cedric like he was an idiot. "I'm not going anywhere. Grab that key. Once I'm free, we'll shift and find your mate. We'll rescue him. We might be small, but it doesn't mean we're helpless."

Cedric sucked in a breath. He hoped his brother was right.

He wasn't sure what would happen if he wasn't, but he supposed they were about to find out.

Jonathan was in trouble. He'd heard the Beasts coming, but he hadn't left. He couldn't, not when Cedric was inside the warehouse. Instead, he'd used himself as a distraction. The Beasts had been talking about someone sneaking around, and he hadn't known whether they'd meant him or Cedric. He couldn't allow them to find his mate, so instead, he'd let them find him.

And now he was inside the warehouse. That was exactly where he'd been planning on going, but not in these circumstances.

"We're going to have so much fun with you," one of the Beasts said.

He looked excited, and Jonathan had no doubt that was exactly the case. He was an enforcer, the Beasts enemy. They wouldn't pull any punches with him.

He hoped Cedric would manage to get his brother out, or at the very least that he would be able to leave and go back to Gillham. Bran had said he would help if they had to, and Jonathan hoped that would be the case. Even if the Beasts started torturing him, they probably wouldn't kill him. They'd want to show Elroy and Rick he was still there when they came back. They were probably proud of having caught him, even though they were idiots and didn't realize he'd *allowed* them to catch him.

"What are you doing here?" another one asked.

"Taking a walk," Jonathan drawled.

The Beast behind him pushed him, and he stumbled. He took a deep breath, not wanting to provoke them. As long as their attention was on him, Cedric was safe, but if he could avoid being beaten, he would.

"Well, you're going to regret taking that walk," the first one said.

He opened one of the doors in the hallway and stepped aside. Jonathan was pushed inside, and he grimaced at the sight that greeted him. This was clearly the cell in which they brought their enemies. There was a lone chair in the middle of it, and if Jonathan wasn't wrong, the dark stains on it were blood. There was blood on the floor, too, and he gritted his teeth.

He was alone. He had no idea what kind of shifter the Beasts were, so he wasn't even sure that shifting into his bear would help. Besides, with Cedric still in the warehouse, he couldn't afford to have the Beasts attention on anything but him. Shifting into a bear would probably achieve that, but it also might push them to kill him, or at least hurt him badly. He needed his strength to fight his way out of here once Cedric was out, though, so he allowed them to push him toward the chair.

He wrinkled his nose when he looked down at it. "I'm not sitting on that."

"You don't have the luxury of choosing where you're sitting." He was pushed, but he resisted. He knew that sitting there would mean torture, and even though he wanted to keep the Beasts' attention on him, he wasn't willing to let himself be tortured. There was no way he'd be able to make it out if they did that to him.

"Do you think we should call Rick?" another Beast asked.

"Are you stupid? He's going to kill us if we distract him. Don't call him. It'll be fine until he comes home."

Jonathan heard soft scuttering, and he frowned, looking around. His eyes widened when he noticed two mice running along the wall. It could be a coincidence. The warehouse seemed to be full of mice, and there was no way this was Cedric and his brother, was there?

Jonathan didn't want to hope, but he also didn't want to think of how much danger Cedric was in if that was him. He was doing this to protect his mate, yet here Cedric was, throwing himself into the path of danger. What was going on in that head of his?

Jonathan suspected he knew. It was the same thing that was going on in *his* head. He could feel how worried Cedric was, and from the way their emotions played through their bond, he was pretty sure that one of the mice was Cedric.

He was proud of his mate for having the courage to do this, but he was also petrified. He couldn't allow the Beasts to hurt Cedric or to put him back in a cell and wait for Rick. He would tear them all apart before it came to that.

The mice came to a stop and turned to look at Jonathan. It only took a few seconds, yet it felt like an eternity. The mouse in the front nodded, and Jonathan nodded back. Then he turned around to face the Beasts behind him.

They were still bickering, but they noticed him moving, and they faced him. The one who'd been trying to get him to sit glared at him. "Sit down and stop fighting if you don't want something bad to happen to you."

Jonathan smiled. It took the Beast aback, and the man took a step back.

Jonathan shifted. He didn't let the Beast move more than the man already had. He reached for him, swiping his paw along the man's face. Blood spurted from the wounds he created, and the man screamed. Jonathan wasn't done with him, though. He swiped his other paw on the man's chest, digging deep, and the Beast fell to the floor, blood dampening the shreds of his t-shirt. Hopefully, he wouldn't get up.

Jonathan turned around to make sure Cedric was okay, and his eyes widened when he saw his mate, in his human form and therefore entirely naked, slamming the chair onto one of the other Beasts' head. The man hadn't seen him coming because he was focused on another naked man, who had to be Archie.

Jonathan could see the resemblance. They looked alike, yet different. Now wasn't the time to think about how much more gorgeous his mate was, though.

Jonathan roared and rushed another Beast. Luckily for them, there were only four in the room, so there wasn't a lot to do. With one of them down for the count thanks to Cedric, Jonathan only had to take care of another two. One of them tried to shift, and from the sight of it, he was pretty sure the man had been a tiger or something that big. Luckily for Jonathan, he got to him before he could do anything, and he managed to knock him down.

Jonathan was breathing hard by the time he was done with the final guy. He was still tense, wondering if other Beasts were going to come, and he jerked when Cedric touched his arm.

Cedric held his hands up. "It's just me. I only counted four of them, so I think that's all."

Jonathan shifted, and before he could do anything else, he dragged Cedric into his arms.

Cedric chuckled and hugged him. "I have to say that this isn't the way I want to be naked with you."

Jonathan couldn't help but laugh. He needed this moment of levity after what had happened and how terrified he'd been. "Don't worry. We can be naked together in any way you want as soon as we get back to Gillham."

Cedric took a step back. "We have to go. They need us."

Jonathan nodded and looked at Archie. "I suppose that's your brother?"

"It is. Archie, this is Jonathan, my mate. Jonathan, Archie. Now let's go. I think I counted the total number of guards, but I could be wrong, and I don't want to risk it. This was terrifying, and I can't go through it a second time."

"You're brave and strong. I'm proud of you."

Cedric blinked, then smiled. "You can tell me all how proud you are of me once we're out of here." He wrinkled his nose. "Although I can't say I'm happy about having to shimmer naked."

Jonathan sighed. "Your clothes are outside, so you're fine. Archie, where are yours?"

"In my cell."

"All right. Go grab them. I'll find something."

"Look upstairs," Archie suggested. "That's where the Beasts are sleeping. I'm sure some of them have clothes that'll fit."

Jonathan took that suggestion and ran with it. He found clothes that were just a bit small in the first bedroom, and he didn't look further than that. He didn't need to. Once he was done, he went back to the brothers, relieved to see they were okay and waiting for him. Together, they stepped out. Cedric had shifted back, but as soon as they got back to his clothes, he became human again and dressed. In the meantime, Jonathan tried calling Nadha, but she wasn't answering.

He stared at his phone, wondering why. "Something's wrong."

"Call one of the Nix services. We have to get back to Gillham," Cedric suggested.

He was right, so Jonathan did just that. He was terrified about what they might find once they got there, and he was right. The Nix shimmered them to the entrance of pack territory, saw what was happening, and immediately shimmered away.

Jonathan didn't have that luxury, though.

He looked around. It was crowded, with everyone fighting everyone. It wasn't easy to recognize the Beasts, not when some of them had shifted into their animal forms. Jonathan didn't know where to start, but he was freaking out about

Cedric and Archie being right in the middle of it.

"Isn't that one of your friends?" Cedric asked.

Jonathan turned to look where Cedric was looking, and his stomach dropped when he saw Tanner leaning against a tree. His arm was hanging down his body, useless, and he was bleeding.

"Shit," Jonathan swore as he rushed to Tanner. He was relieved to see that Cedric and Archie were coming after him. He couldn't leave them alone. "Tanner. Talk to me." Tanner wasn't one of Jonathan's team members anymore, but he had been when Jonathan had first become an enforcer. He was human, but he was an enforcer, and it was obvious he'd been fighting.

"I'll be fine." Tanner's gaze moved behind Jonathan. "You should take them away from here."

"Only if you come with me, too."

"I have to help."

"You won't be able to do much with that arm. Come on. Let's find a healer, or at least a Nix. Once that's done, you can go back to the fight."

Someone cried out behind Jonathan, and he turned to see a lion stalking them. Cedric and Archie were between Jonathan and the lion, so he couldn't do anything. He was afraid to move. He was going to have to, though.

He left Tanner leaning against a tree and grabbed his mate. He pushed Cedric behind him, and luckily, Archie went with him. Before Jonathan could shift, though, a cat jumped onto the lion's head.

Jonathan blinked, wondering what was going on. He didn't know any cat shifters in the enforcers, although he could be wrong. Who knew who Bran had brought in from other towns?

Whoever that was, it didn't matter. The cat was giving them the opportunity to run away, and they had to take it.

Jonathan turned to tell Cedric and the others exactly that, but as he opened his mouth, a searing pain burned through his thigh. He swung around, already shifting, and knocked the hyena shifter off his body. The hyena hit a tree and didn't get up, but the damage was done. Jonathan's knees buckled, and he fell to the ground.

Cedric cried out and rushed to him. Jonathan wanted to shift and reassure him, but he couldn't. He had to protect his mate and his friends. It wasn't just because he was an enforcer, either. It was because he cared about them, and he wanted them to be okay.

With his thigh feeling like it was on fire, he dragged himself closer to Cedric. He knew he wouldn't be getting back to his feet, but that didn't mean he couldn't defend his mate.

Jonathan was sacrificing himself to protect Cedric and the others, and Cedric couldn't allow that.

He looked around. Everyone was still fighting, including the cat, who was trying to claw the lion's eyes out. No one was paying attention to Cedric and his friends, and Cedric had to do something.

He turned to Archie. "Help me."

Archie's eyes were wide, but he nodded. They both reached for Jonathan, who couldn't protest since he was in his bear form. Cedric was glad, because he knew his mate would have. He wanted to protect Cedric, which made sense, but the other way around was also true. Jonathan had been hurt protecting Cedric, and Cedric would protect him, too.

Jonathan was heavy, though. It was hard for Cedric and Archie to drag him, but thankfully, Jonathan's friend helped. Cedric didn't know him well since they'd only met once a few days ago. They'd been working together to secure the pack against the attack, but Tanner had seemed nice. He was obviously in pain, but he was still helping, and Cedric was grateful. The problem was that he had no idea where they needed to take Jonathan. The entire area was full of fights and no place to hide, and it felt impossible.

"Lean him against a tree," Tanner said.

Cedric obeyed. Tanner was an enforcer, so he knew better than Cedric.

They settled Jonathan against a tree. Cedric could have sworn Jonathan was glaring, but he didn't pay much attention to it. "What now?" he asked.

Tanner straightened his shoulders. He grimaced as he did so, and he was pale, but he seemed convinced of what he was doing. "Now, we defend him. One of you could try finding a Nix, but I doubt he'll be happy about it. Besides, they're no doubt busy."

Cedric swallowed. He wasn't going to let Archie dive into the fight, even if it was to find a Nix to heal Jonathan. He turned his attention to Jonathan. "You think you can make it even if we don't find a healer right away?"

Jonathan nodded. He was bleeding from his thigh, so Cedric he took his t-shirt off and tried to staunch the blood flow as much as he could. He doubted it would work in the long run, but for now it was better than nothing.

He, Archie, and Tanner stood shoulder to shoulder, surrounding Jonathan, who was grumbling. Cedric was terrified. He didn't want to lose anyone, not even Tanner, but he knew how likely that was to happen.

"Who was that cat shifter?" Archie asked.

"No idea," Tanner said. "He was brave, though."

"He jumped on the lion shifter as if he wasn't just a cat."

"And he saved us in the process."

Cedric agreed. He didn't have time to tell them that, though, because a wolf rushed toward them. He wasn't sure the wolf was friend or foe, but Tanner didn't take the time to ask. As soon as the wolf reached them, he punched it with his good hand. Cedric sucked in a breath, but he had to help. He didn't know how. He wouldn't be of any use if he shifted, so he had to stick to his human form.

He looked around, located a branch that had fallen from a tree, and grabbed it. When the wolf tried to charge them again, he swung it like a baseball bat. It hit the wolf right on the face, and Cedric winced when he heard a crunch. The wolf dropped, leaving Cedric there, heaving.

"Come back here," Tanner said.

Cedric nodded and moved back to the little group. That was when he noticed something happening not far from them. Kameron and Bran were standing there, facing Elroy.

Cedric sucked in a breath. "Look," he murmured.

The other three turned to look at what he was watching. Why wasn't Elroy attacking? What were they doing?

"He's having his villain moment," Archie said.

"He can't be that stupid, can he?" Tanner asked.

Cedric was pretty sure he was.

"You killed my brother!" Elroy yelled.

Kameron didn't seem to understand what he was talking about. "Who was your brother?"

"He was an alpha in LA. Alpha Kramer. You killed him. You dismantled his pack."

Kam shook his head. "Is that why you're here? I didn't kill your brother. I had nothing to do with his death."

"I don't believe you."

"I don't care what you believe." Kameron shifted. Elroy barely had time to react. Kameron was on him in seconds.

Cedric heard someone cry out. It was a young man who tried to rush into the fight, but Bran grabbed him and pulled him back.

"That's Kameron's son," Tanner explained.

Cedric grimaced. He hoped the man wouldn't have to

watch his father being killed. He had to have faith. Kameron was strong, and he was a fighter. He would kick Elroy's ass. Then the pack would take care of the remaining Beasts, and everyone would be safe and happy.

Cedric had to believe that.

Elroy shifted, too, and the two wolves faced each other. It was easy to identify them. Elroy's wolf was battered, with scars that ran down his sides and his face. Even when they jumped on each other in a flurry of snarls and bites, Cedric could keep track.

He was pretty sure he held his breath the entire time.

Kameron took a bite out of one of Elroy's ears, but it didn't stop Elroy. Elroy launched himself toward Kameron, aiming for his neck. Kameron sidestepped him, using a paw to trip him and send him to the ground. Elroy rolled and got back to his feet. He didn't pause and jumped on Kameron again, managing to bite his shoulder. Blood spurted, but it didn't slow Kameron down. He pushed back, knocking Elroy down. Once Elroy was sprawled out, Kameron moved until he was on top of him. He grabbed Elroy's neck with his teeth, then stopped moving.

Cedric stared. He understood why Kameron wasn't killing Elroy, but he desperately wanted him to. He wanted revenge for what had been done to him, even though Rick had been the one to torture him and Archie, not Elroy. Still, they wouldn't have been in this situation if Elroy wasn't around. Cedric wanted Elroy to die, as well as Rick.

Bran stepped forward. "You can surrender and end all of this. Call your Beasts back. You'll go to jail, but you'll be alive."

Cedric knew what Elroy's answer would be even before Elroy snarled and tried to buck Kameron off his body. Instead of moving, Kameron tightened his hold on Elroy's neck.

The snap was audible, and it made Cedric wince. He'd

wanted this, but he wasn't happy about anyone dying. Now that Elroy was gone, though, the world would be a safer place for everyone, including him in his brother.

Elroy's body slumped on the ground, and Kameron stepped away. He shifted, then, seemingly uncaring that he was naked, looked around.

Cedric and his friends weren't the only ones who'd stopped to watch the fight. Once the Beasts realized what had happened, they started running. A few stayed, but with Elroy gone, as well as many of their friends, there was little they could do, and they were captured. Some had died, but Cedric wouldn't mourn them.

"What do you think happened to Rick?" he asked Archie.

Archie shook his head. "I don't know, but if there's anyone who made it out alive, it's him."

"We'll make sure he never hurts you again," Jonathan said from behind them.

Cedric twirled around to face his mate. "What are you doing? You should be down there resting." Jonathan was heavily leaning against the tree, but he was on his feet.

"I'm okay. But I promise you that if Rick isn't one of the Beasts who died today, I'll find him, and I'll make sure he pays for what he did to the two of you."

Cedric shook his head. "That won't be necessary. I'm sure he's dead." He had to be. A lot of Beasts were on the ground, and Cedric wanted to go through all of them and find Rick. He had to focus on Jonathan, though. He'd left Rick behind, and Cedric knew that even if Rick *was* alive, he'd never go back to him.

Instead of doing what he wanted and looking for Rick, he moved toward Jonathan. "Sit down. I'll get you a healer."

Jonathan glared at him. "I'm never going to win any discussion with you, am I?"

"Not when you're so obviously wrong."

CHAPTER SEVEN

Jonathan glared down at his thigh. It was mostly healed, so why was it still weak? Why was he being forced to stay in bed?

Okay, so maybe that last part was all Cedric. Dallas and Sei had been around, and while Dallas had told Jonathan to rest as much as possible, he hadn't mentioned anything about staying in bed. Cedric had insisted, though, and Jonathan already couldn't deny him anything. Still, he'd had enough of this bedroom. He wanted to go out. He wanted to help clean up the bodies and the blood. He wanted to be there to honor the enforcers who had fallen. Instead, he was stuck in bed, and it was his mate's fault.

Jonathan had enough, though. He pushed the blankets back and swung his legs to the floor. He got to his feet, only for his knees to buckle. He tilted forward, slamming against the floor and barely managing to put his hands up to protect his face.

"What was that noise?" he heard Cedric ask from the bedroom door.

Jonathan groaned and rolled to his back. His mate was going to yell at him, and apparently, he wouldn't be. Maybe Jonathan should have stayed in bed, since he wasn't even able to take one step without falling on his face.

Cedric rushed in, freezing when he saw Jonathan on the floor. "What are you doing?"

Jonathan rolled his head to look at Cedric. "What does it look like I'm doing? I fell."

Cedric glared and put his hands on his hips. "And how did you fall?"

"I tried to get up."

Cedric rolled his eyes. "Of course you did. I don't know if I can carry you back to bed. I might have to call someone."

"Please don't. Just give me a hand, and I'll shuffle around until I'm on the bed again."

Cedric didn't look convinced, but thankfully, he obeyed. It took a bit for him to get Jonathan back on his feet, but Jonathan helped, using his good leg and his hands, along with the bed. Once he was on his feet again, he had to take a deep breath. He felt shaky, and he realized that he probably shouldn't have tried to get out of bed.

"Are you going to listen to the doctor now?" Cedric asked.

"Technically, I didn't *not* listen to him. He never said I had to stay in bed."

"You think you're funny? Because you're not."

"I'm bored. I don't want to have to look at the same four walls anymore."

"You've only been here since yesterday. What are you talking about?"

"It's still too long."

Cedric helped Jonathan sit back on the bed, then pulled the blankets on top of his legs again. Jonathan sighed heavily and leaned back against the pillows. He couldn't deny he felt better now that he was sitting down.

"I understand what you're going through," Cedric murmured. "You want to help. You want to see what's going on outside. You want to go to pack territory and make sure everyone is okay. You can't leave this bed, though. But if you want, I can make some calls and get your team here."

Jonathan found himself smiling. "That would be great." He knew all his members had made it out of the fight in one piece, but he still wanted to see them and reassure himself they really were okay.

Nadha had been wounded, which was why she hadn't answered the phone when Jonathan had called her. She'd been unconscious. She would be fine, though. Lorcan had suffered claw marks to his chest and back, and they would leave scars, but he would be okay, too. They all would, even Tanner. That was all Jonathan had been able to get out of Dallas, but he needed more information. He wanted to make sure Tanner would be able to use his arm again. Dallas had warned Jonathan that he might walk with a limp from now on, but Jonathan would do everything he could to make sure that didn't happen.

He was an enforcer. It was his job to protect people, and he wouldn't be able to do that if he had a limp.

Cedric sat on the edge of the mattress. "Will you allow me to take care of you if I call your friends?"

"I don't need you to take care of me. I should be out there cleaning up the town and pack territory."

Cedric shook his head. "You can't. You can't even get to the bathroom without falling. What do you think you could do out there?"

Jonathan looked away. Cedric was right, but he felt useless. He'd been useless in the fight, too. He'd been wounded almost as soon as he'd arrived, and he hadn't been able to do anything else. He supposed he should be grateful he'd at least protected Cedric and Archie.

He felt the mattress dip as Cedric climbed up so he could settle against Jonathan's side. Jonathan hooked an arm around Cedric's shoulders and held him close while Cedric wrapped himself around him as well as he could without touching his thigh.

"I know you don't like being stuck here," Cedric said softly. "If you weren't hurt, you would be out there helping your friends. You have to stay, though. I don't want you to get hurt even more than you already are. I don't think I would be able to take it."

Jonathan sucked in a breath. He hadn't even thought about what it would have felt like for Cedric to watch that hyena hurt him. "I'll be fine. You heard Dallas. I need a few more healing sessions from Sei, but I'll be okay."

"I know. You have to be careful, though. You'll worsen the wound. Sei will already have a hard enough time healing you. Besides, I don't know if I can let you out of my sight right now. Every time I close my eyes, I see that hyena attacking you. I'm terrified of losing you, and I'm not sorry about it."

Jonathan kissed the top of Cedric's head. "You don't have to be sorry. I was terrified for you, too. I'm glad you made it out without being hurt."

"I'm glad, too, but I'm worried about you. Stay in bed for a bit. Besides, I doubt that the cleaning will be done in one day. As soon as you're on your feet again, you can go. In the meantime, though, humor me. Please."

Jonathan could only agree. He would do pretty much everything for his mate. He was falling in love with Cedric, and even though he was grumpy about having to stay in bed, this felt like a new start for both of them.

Cedric was strong, resilient, and loving. He was brave. He'd stepped in to protect Jonathan even though he'd been terrified, and he wouldn't have been able to do much against the Beasts. Still, he'd been willing to sacrifice himself for his brother and for Jonathan. It meant a lot, but it was only one of the reasons Jonathan was falling for his mate.

He knew Cedric could feel the affection he had for him through the bond, but thankfully, he didn't bring it up. They were both a little vulnerable, a little too raw, to talk about it. Eventually, they would, but not today.

Cedric wasn't going anywhere. The Beasts had finally been dealt with. Elroy was dead, as was Rick, who had been found in town. No one knew who had killed him, but it didn't matter, not as long as he was dead and would never be able to hurt Archie and Cedric again. It would take a while to clean up, and everyone was traumatized, but they would survive.

Gillham was strong, as were the people who lived there. They would deal with the trauma, and they would get back on their feet. Jonathan was glad he and Cedric would be building a life here.

It wouldn't be easy, but then, nothing worth having ever was. Jonathan and everyone else were willing to fight for Gillham, but now, Jonathan had even more to fight for. He had his mate, his friends, and even a brother-in-law.

"I'm glad you're okay," Cedric murmured.

"I'm glad you're okay, too."

"I don't think it's wise," Morven said. He was doing his best not to glare at Orran, but he knew he was failing.

Orran crossed his arms over his chest. "The queen okayed it."

"It doesn't mean it's wise."

"What would you have him do?"

"He left his family behind. It should be a clean break."

Blake cleared his throat. "I understand what you're saying, but I can't let my brother think I'm dead. The queen said I could call him, and I will. It's just to reassure him that I'm okay and to tell him that he won't see me again."

Morven understood why Blake wanted to do that, but he thought it was a stupid idea. He'd known what he was doing when he'd agreed to leave the human world behind and stay with the dragons. He'd chosen this, and he had to go along with it. Instead, here he was, about to call his brother and tell him he was fine. "Will you explain about dragons?" he asked.

Blake shook his head. "I promised I wouldn't. I'm not an

idiot."

"I never said you were. But this is your brother we're talking about. It's one of the people you're closest to, isn't he?"

Blake's gaze flickered to Orran, and Morven almost rolled his eyes. "He is. He's the person I was the closest to until I met Orran. That's why I owe it to him to explain what happened."

"You're going to give him hope. Wouldn't it be better for him to think you're dead?"

"I can't let that happen. Sheldon was there for me when I needed him, and I know that right now, he's frantic. He's going to do something stupid to try to find me, and I can't let that happen. I promise I won't tell him where I am or about you guys. I just want him to know I'm fine."

Morven sighed. "It's not like I can forbid you to do it anyway."

"I know. I just don't want you to hate me."

Morven blinked. "Why would I hate you?"

Blake stared at him. "You're serious right now? Why wouldn't you hate me? I know you're Orran's best friend, and you were the one closest to him until I arrived. I know you don't trust me because I'm human."

"That's not true. I never said I didn't trust you."

"But you're not trusting him with this," Orran pointed out.

Sometimes, Morven wanted to strangle his best friend. "It's not that I don't trust you," he repeated, looking at Blake. "It's that it's dangerous. I know the queen told you that you could do this, but her family is still trying to knock her off the throne. They're not the only ones, either. Several of the clans have learned about your presence here, and they're using it as proof that the queen is weak. If she can't even keep a human out of the clan, who's to say that she's a good clan leader and that we can withstand attacks?"

Blake bit his lower lip. "I don't want to put the clan in danger, and I know that even only my presence here does. I need to talk to Sheldon, though."

Morven could tell he wouldn't change Blake's mind. "Then

call him. Explain what happened. As long as you remember that you can't tell him much, I won't say anything."

"You've already said plenty."

"Nothing I said made you change your mind. Besides, the queen agreed to this. Her orders take precedent to mine."

Blake grinned and looked down at his phone. It had been turned off since he and Orran had been on the run, and it was obvious he couldn't wait to turn it on again. Morven might think this was a bad idea, but he could understand where Blake was coming from.

He didn't know what he would do if he couldn't tell Orran or any of his other friends that he was okay. He could only imagine how Orran would feel if he thought he was dead. He would try to find him, no matter the consequences, and from what Blake was saying, the same went for his brother. Of course, Blake's brother was human, so there probably wasn't much he could do to find him, but he could put himself in danger. Blake would never forgive himself if something happened to his brother because of this, and Morven suspected that neither would Orran.

Blake lifted the phone to his ear and waited. Morven held his breath, even though he didn't much care about the outcome of this. He only cared that Blake was putting them in danger. Hopefully, he was as trustworthy as the queen and Orran thought he was—and his brother would be, too.

"Blake?" a voice asked.

Morven glared at the phone. His brother had yelled so loudly that even Morven had heard it, and he wasn't anywhere close to Blake.

"Yeah, it's me," Blake answered.

Morven didn't hear what Blake's brother answered, but he could imagine. He should probably listen in to the conversation, but even though he couldn't believe he felt like this, he did trust Blake not to say anything that pertained to the dragons or the palace. Instead, he turned his attention to Orran.

Orran wasn't head of security anymore. He was a tutor,

and as such, he wasn't privy to the information Morven had. He'd been head of security for years, though, while Morven had only just started. He could do with some help, or at the very least, advice.

The queen had been threatened, which was nothing new. Still, it made Morven nervous. He knew a lot of dragons were going to try to use the fact that Blake was staying with them and was the queen's son's tutor against her. If they could topple her off the throne, they would. If that happened, they would probably kill Blake and anyone who stood in their path to him, and that included Orran.

Morven might not understand it, but he knew Orran loved Blake, and that nothing would change that. That meant that if Blake was threatened, Orran would step in, and Morven didn't want that to happen. He didn't want to lose his best friend, and even more importantly, he didn't want anything to happen to the queen.

She was a good leader. Her father had been before her, and a lot of elders hadn't liked the fact that she was a female. Her father hadn't seen anything wrong with that, and he'd taught her out to be a good leader. When he died, she took his place, even though some elders had tried to convince her otherwise. They'd thought she would make a good queen, but only at the side of a king.

The queen had told them to take a hike.

That was where the displeasure and hate against her were rooted, and Morven knew some people would take advantage of the fact that Blake was there.

"Thank you," Orran murmured.

When Morven looked at him, he was staring at Blake, who was still on the phone. "What are you thanking me for?"

"For allowing him to do this. I know the queen told him he could, but I'm sure that if you told her it was too dangerous, she would forbid it."

"I don't hate Blake, and I don't want him to stay away from his family. It's a necessity, though."

Orran turned his gaze toward Morven. "How are things going?"

It made Morven smile. "You're not head of security anymore, remember?"

"How could I not? You don't miss a chance to remind me of it. The fact that I'm not head of security anymore doesn't mean I can't advise you, though. I also want to know what's going on. I have to protect Blake."

Morven sighed. "Nothing new. The queen has been threatened, and people aren't happy about Blake's presence here. It's mostly the elders, but you know someone is going to take advantage of this sooner or later."

"I'm aware." He looked at Blake again. "I can't give him up, though."

"I know. I'm not asking you to." Because Morven knew that if he did, he'd lose. If Blake had to leave, he had no doubt that Orran would go with him. He might not understand it, but it was clear as day, and he wasn't going to risk it. His friendship with Orran was important to him, and just as Orran would do everything he could to keep Blake safe, Morven would do the same for Orran.

Sheldon didn't know what to think. He wasn't even sure he could think, not with Blake on the other side of the phone. "Where are you? I'll pick you up."

Blake chuckled. "Still trying to mother me, I see."

"I'm not mothering you. I'm offering you a ride. That's it."

"We both know that's not true, but fine. I'll play along." He sighed so heavily that Sheldon could hear him for the phone. "And you can't pick me up."

"Why not? What happened to you? I've been trying to call you for days, and you never answered." It was closer to weeks, but Sheldon didn't want Blake to think he truly was overbearing. He probably was, but who could blame him? He and Blake only had each other.

"I met someone."

Sheldon blinked. That was not what he thought he'd hear. "You disappeared for weeks because you met a guy?"

Blake huffed. "Okay, said like that, it sounds bad. Hear me out, though."

"I'm listening, but you better give me a good reason for me not to find you wherever you are and kick your ass."

"Like I said, I met someone. A guy. He's incredible. I can't believe I was that lucky, and I'm with him right now."

"Okay. So you don't want me to pick you up. I still want to see you."

"It's not going to be possible. I'm not in the city anymore."

Sheldon had to swallow twice before he was able to speak again. "You left the city without telling me?"

"I'm sorry. I didn't mean for anything like this to happen, but I didn't have the time to warn you."

"So you're with him now?"

"I am. And I can never come back, Sheldon."

Sheldon couldn't think. He heard the words, but they didn't make sense. "What does that even mean?"

"I can't explain. The only thing I can tell you is that I'm safe and happy. I'm in love, and I hope that now that you know I'm fine, you'll be able to go on with your life. I know you were worried about me. You don't have to be, though."

"Is he forcing you?"

"What are you talking about?"

"You just said that you met someone and that you can never come back. Is he keeping you prisoner?" It was that or Blake was lying to Sheldon, and Sheldon didn't want that to be the case.

He wanted his brother to trust him the way he'd always trusted Blake. They might have grown distant in the past few years, but it was only because of the circumstances they were in, not because Sheldon didn't love his brother anymore or because he didn't trust him.

"I'm not a prisoner. I promise you I'm safe and happy.

Please, Sheldon. I can't explain."

Sheldon was already thinking about who this mystery guy could be. As far as he knew, Blake didn't have friends. He didn't go out much except for work, which meant that whoever this guy was, Blake had probably met him at the bar where he'd been working. "You won't tell me anything else?" he asked because he had to try.

"I told you what I could. Just be happy for me. I'm sorry I had to leave you behind, and if I could change things, I would. I can't, though. That means that we can't see each other again, but we can talk on the phone."

"I suppose that's better than nothing."

Sheldon could almost hear the wincing in Blake's voice. "I know you're angry."

"You're damn right I'm angry. You disappear for weeks without telling anyone what happened to you, and when you finally call me, it's only to tell me that you met someone and that we can never see each other again. It doesn't make sense. Are you in a cult? Are you lying?"

"I'm not."

"You're not telling me everything, though. That's a lie by omission."

"I'm telling you what I can. Please, Sheldon. This is important to me. I need you to stay away. You can't try to find me. You wouldn't be able to anyway, and I don't want you to get in trouble. I called you because I wanted you to know I was fine."

"You're not fine. If you can't tell me what's going on, I'll have to find out on my own."

"You're infuriating. You can't find out on your own. You're going to get hurt, and it'll be your fault because you wouldn't listen to me. Can't you do that for once?"

"You left me!" Sheldon sucked in a breath. He hadn't meant to burst out the way he had, but it wasn't a lie.

Blake was silent for a moment, and Sheldon wondered if he'd hung up. He tightened his hold on the phone and waited.

"I'm sorry," Blake finally said. "I never wanted to leave you. You know what my life was like, though. You have your job and a family, but I had nothing."

"My job is boring, and our family would hate me if they knew."

"What are you talking about?"

Sheldon shook his head even though Blake couldn't see him. "Never mind that. They kicked you out. They act as if you never existed. I don't care if I have them. I don't want them. I want you."

"I'm touched, but it's better this way. Now, you know I'm happy. I have my own life. I have a job and a man I love."

"And you're leaving me behind for that."

"I wouldn't if I didn't have to. You have to believe that."

"How can I believe it when I have no idea what's happening?"

"This is all I can tell you. I'm sorry, Sheldon. I hope you'll understand eventually."

Sheldon knew what Blake was doing. "Don't you dare hang up on me. You have no right to. I want answers, and you're going to give them to me."

But Sheldon could already hear the beeping that told him that Blake had hung up.

He lowered his phone and stared at it. Then, he blindly sat onto the couch.

He was glad his brother was okay, but he was also worried. Something was happening for Blake to tell him that he couldn't see him ever again. Sheldon didn't know what it was, but he would find out. He wasn't abandoning Blake. Their family already had, but Sheldon was different. His brother needed him. Even if he wasn't lying, he wasn't telling Sheldon everything, which meant something was going on. Blake might still be in danger, and Sheldon had to do something about it.

What, though? He wasn't going just to accept the fact that they couldn't see each other again without fighting. Blake should have known that, and maybe he had. He wasn't wrong when he said that Sheldon had no way to find him, though. Sheldon didn't even know where to start.

He'd gone to Blake's apartment, but Blake hadn't been there. The place had been abandoned, and Sheldon had had to pack his brother's things and put them away when the landlord had realized Blake wouldn't be back. The boxes were still in his living room, where he could see them every day.

The only other place he knew where to look was the bar were Blake had worked. Sheldon didn't want to go there, but he knew he was going to have to. No matter how little he liked it, it was his only link to his brother, and he wouldn't waste it. He was going to find Blake whether Blake liked it or not.

ABOUT THE AUTHOR

Catherine is the creator of several series, most of them paranormal, including the Whitedell Pride Series and the Gillham Pack Series. While she graduated in translation, she decided to go the writer's way because it was more fun to create her own stories and characters.

She's been living in Italy for more than twenty years, but she's a daughter of the North—Belgium to be precise—and she misses it so much that she's already planning to move back.

She loves pizza—probably too much—her son, her pets, and of course, books. She sneaks some reading time into her schedule every time she has five minutes free from writing, demands from her various pets and son, and lastly, housework.

Connect with her:

lievens.catherine@gmail.com
BookBub: https://www.bookbub.com/authors/catherine-lievens
Website: https://authorcatherinelievens.com/
Facebook: https://www.facebook.com/catherine.lievens.9
Facebook Group: https://www.facebook.com/groups/411788002341528/
Twitter: https://twitter.com/authorCLievens
Newsletter: http://eepurl.com/c-uvKn

www.ingramcontent.com/pod-product-compliance
Lightning Source LLC
Chambersburg PA
CBHW060614130626
46555CB00002B/520